Lancashire
Hotpot Peril

Albert Smith's Culinary Capers

Recipe 9

Steve Higgs

Dedication

I wish life was like a bowl of stew,
Chuck in the ingredients,
A pint of affection or two,
give it a stir,
Stand back, just wait,
Voila, life, served on a plate,

Or is it more like soufflé, a delicate dish,
The ingredients can be right,
But the result, not what you wish,
If it peaks too fast,
Goes way past it's best,
It gets thrown away, along with the rest.

Sell me the recipe,
Show me the book,
I'll pay for expensive truffles,
If you just let me look,
Give me a clue how life's dish is served best,
Tell me the precise contents,
I'll put it to the test.

I think it's hot pot,
You just put stuff in a pan,
You stir it around,
Do the best you can,
What comes out you'll never really know,
Until you taste it,
Let its flavour show.
Then adjust the recipe, add pinches of spice
Then maybe you'll find,
Life's really very nice.

Table of Contents:

A Scent on the Breeze

A light autumn drizzle dampened Albert's hair, skin and clothing as the bus pulled away. The same rain fell on Rex's coat, forming tiny globules of water until they grew heavy enough to roll off.

Rex shook himself, ridding his fur of the annoying moisture and looked up at the grey clouds above. There was blue sky in the near distance, moving their way as the clouds rolled along.

'It looks set to be a nice day, boy,' commented Albert as he adjusted the pack on his shoulders and picked up his small suitcase.

They were in the Lancashire town of Clitheroe, arriving after a day of travelling from Dundee by train and then by bus. Due to work on the line, they'd been forced to disembark two stations early and make the final miles on a bus. Supplied by the rail line, taking the bus, and the delay doing so incurred, was nothing more than a minor inconvenience, though some of the other passengers grumbled and groaned as if they were being asked to donate a vital organ.

It made little difference to Albert. It was mid-afternoon, which for a man who set his clock by his mealtimes, meant it was roughly halfway between luncheon and dinner.

Rex, on the other hand, believed any time of the day was a perfect time to eat dinner. Or breakfast, or elevenses. He truly didn't care which meal it was, so long as it happened. His nose was in the air now, held upward despite the light raindrops falling on it.

They were somewhere new and that meant there were new smells to identify and learn. The dominant smell in the air was Hotpot, the dish the county of Lancashire was arguably most famous for.

Unnoticed by Rex, Albert had his nose in the air too. So far as the dog was concerned, noses on humans were for decoration only. He was wrong though, they worked perfectly well, just not at the same level he was accustomed to.

As a former police dog, the oversized German Shepherd's nose was more attuned than your average household pet. Sniffing the same air as his human, he could detect individual herbs, black pepper, carrot, and potato ... the list went on.

Albert couldn't do that. But he could smell Hotpot and it made his stomach rumble. Suddenly hungry, even though he knew he shouldn't be, Albert discarded his plan to find his hotel and went in search of the award-winning restaurant that caused his pilgrimage.

'Come along, Rex,' he chimed cheerfully. 'I dare say you and I could afford a small portion to keep the cold at bay.'

In truth, it wasn't all that cold. Albert just wanted to taste the dish he came here for. Walking in the direction his mental map of the town insisted was the right one, he checked both ways and crossed the road. *Is this my eighth stop?* he wondered as he stepped back onto the pavement on the other side of the road, *or my ninth or tenth?*

Following his nose as much as the map in his head, Albert tried to work out how many places he had now stopped at. A little more than a month ago, on the anniversary of his wife's death, he'd chosen to set out on an adventure.

The intention was to journey around the British Isles, stopping in towns made famous by a dish. Many of those dishes carried the name of the town they came from: Bakewell pudding, Stilton cheese, Dundee cake ... However, a day into the first leg of his trip, the seventy-eight-year-old retired senior police detective found himself unintentionally embroiled in a murder investigation.

Nothing much had changed since.

He needed to use his fingers in the end but counted to nine, three times to be sure he hadn't missed a stop somewhere.

Rex could smell a lady spaniel in season, a spill of milk across the road, and a pub with the door open to let the beer fumes coming off the carpet waft out. The pub was farther up the road, about a hundred yards distant still. He liked going into pubs; there was always food on the floor if he smelled hard enough.

However, the promise of a bowl of hotpot – he understood his human's words well enough – sounded vastly superior to some pork rind or potato crisp crumbs licked off the carpet. Rex didn't need a map to find the restaurant they were going to. He didn't even need eyes. His nose would get him there more assuredly than a GPS guided by a satellite in space.

Biting his lip when they reached a junction, Albert could not now remember which way he needed to turn.

Rex tugged at his arm. 'You want the restaurant, right? It's this way.'

Albert glanced at his dog but resisted being led anywhere because a woman was coming his way. She was on his side of the road and had bags of shopping from a local supermarket just along the road. To Albert's cop brain, that made her a local and thus a perfect source of information.

'Excuse me,' he hallooed as she came near. He was all but blocking her path with Rex at his side. 'Can you tell me where I might find Parsons' Perfect Hotpots?'

Rex tugged at his human's arm again. 'It's just along here. Use your nose, man.'

The lady, unhappy about being forced to stay out in the rain any longer than was absolutely necessary, sided with the dog.

'You can see it from here.' She nodded along the road.

When Albert squinted where she was looking, she went around him, hurrying on her way. He called out to thank her and followed the direction she indicated.

Rex quickened his pace. The clouds were having one last go before they left the town behind, increasing their drizzle to something close to a downpour.

Albert was beginning to wish he'd put his hat on. He had too little hair for it to provide much absorbency, so the cold drops hitting his head were rolling off his scalp to dampen his shirt collar. Soon it wouldn't be damp, it would be soaked; the wet patch extending down his torso if he didn't get out of the rain or find some protection from it.

Mercifully, he spied the restaurant.

Hurrying the last few yards, his tastebuds were revving up for the tasty dish he was going to find inside. There would be no need for a menu for he knew precisely what he was going to order.

However, as he reached out to grab the door handle, the door opened inward, and a hand came out to stop him entering.

Albert's eyes ran along the hand and onto the arm where he saw instantly the distinct insignia of a police constable.

'Sorry, sir. The premises are shut for the rest of the day. You'll have to come back tomorrow.'

Scarcely able to believe his ears, Albert's jaw flapped up and down a couple of times without any words coming out. He could smell the hotpot, yet he was to be denied it?

Before he could think of anything to say, the police officer stepped out into the rain. Using both arms to force Albert backward without physically touching him, he made way for people inside to leave.

'Sir, I'll need you to step away now.'

Albert wanted to question what might have befallen the restaurant, but he saw for himself in the next second as two men in coroner's clothing exited the front door of the establishment with a stretcher between them.

On the stretcher was a black body bag and there was someone inside it.

'Clear the way, sir.' The police officer repeated his previous instruction with a little more force behind his words. It was enough to jolt Albert from his reverie.

He tugged at Rex's lead, stepping backward and out of the way so the men with their terrible and heavy load could pass. The coroner's van was right there at the roadside, not five yards away. In his haste to get to the restaurant, and buoyed along by the glorious smell, he completely failed to notice.

He hadn't even seen the two police squad cars parked opposite.

A frustrated breath escaped the old man's lips. He had been so close to sampling what was supposed to be the nation's best version of one of his favourite dishes. There remained a niggling concern that he might think his wife's hotpot to be superior, but then ... were that the case, he could accept how lucky he had been to eat it all those years.

Whether it proved to be superior or not. He wasn't going to sample it today.

The constable caught Albert's attention again. 'Move along, please, sir.'

Albert let a frown crease his brow. He was standing on the pavement, a public right of way, and in no way obstructing the officer in his duties. He had every right to refuse to move, yet he knew from lengthy experience, how much easier it was to disperse a crowd of curious onlookers if one never allowed them to form in the first place.

In that moment when he argued with himself about how he ought to react, he noted how scruffy the officer was. Indeed, Albert could not recall ever seeing one so slovenly. The man was six feet four inches tall by Albert's reckoning, with dark brown hair well overdue a cut. His uniform didn't fit him, most especially the tunic, the buttons of which were strained to breaking point.

A voice from the past – one of his superiors back when Albert had been a constable – surfaced in his head. It laughed in his memory, claiming the man looked like a snake had swallowed a hippo. It was cruel, but also rather accurate.

Dismissing the constable, who was now texting on his phone and paying zero attention to his duties, Albert took a final gaze through the windows of the restaurant, longingly savouring the heavenly scent filling his nostrils. Accepting defeat, he turned away.

'Come along, Rex.'

Rex had been waiting patiently, unsure what the delay to going inside might be. He also had the scent of food in his nostrils. Now his human was trying to take him in the other direction.

He dug his paws in.

'Excuse me? I thought we had this plan for how we were not going to be outside in the rain. Did it not also involve us being inside eating food?'

'Come along, Rex,' Albert coaxed his dog who was being uncharacteristically stubborn.

Grumpily, Rex eased his muscles and went the way his human wanted to go.

'Okay, old man, but I hope there is food in this direction too.'

Sadly, for Rex, there wasn't. Unable to get the dish he'd come here for, Albert had no desire to try a pale imitation elsewhere. Other establishments might produce a tasty hotpot, but he wanted the one deemed worthy of multiple awards.

Telling his stomach and taste buds to calm themselves, he reorientated himself and set off for his hotel. Habitually, Albert selected a cheap, no frills, bed and breakfast. He liked small family-run places where he would meet the owner and he wholeheartedly believed they took personal pride in delivering a service with a personal touch that one just didn't find with larger establishments.

However, his trip around Britain had not gone to plan, and making a last moment decision to visit Clitheroe he found there were no rooms to be had. None anywhere.

Well, almost.

He learned when he asked the fifth or sixth bed and breakfast owner to report they were full, that there was an event in the town the day he wanted to visit. A TV chef was putting on a live cooking and tasting event in the town square that evening. Albert knew the man – *Chris Caan Cooks* was a TV show Petunia used to watch. Albert had even paid attention himself a few times.

There were posters at the train station, and on bus stops as he walked through the Lancashire town. All displayed Chris Caan's smiling face and today's date.

It had been luck that he found a hotel with an available suite. It wasn't a franchise place – one of those soulless cookie-cutter places that charged a pittance and offered even less. He would have simply changed his plans had that been the case. The suite was about four times what he might have paid at a bed and breakfast, but he wasn't short of money, and at seventy-eight, he was quite conscious that he couldn't take it with him.

It was a short walk, but quite far enough in the rain. Located next to a brewery, it proved easy to find as it was signposted.

However, as he turned the final corner to bring him into the street with his hotel, a sense of déjà-vu made his eyes bug out.

There were police cars parked outside the hotel entrance and an officer standing at the door. Incredulously, Albert saw as he came nearer, it was the same scruffy individual who barred his entrance to Parsons' Perfect Hotpots.

The constable's face clouded as Albert crossed the road and made a beeline for the hotel.

'I'm staying here,' Albert called out loud enough for the man to hear. 'Or, I should say I am booked in to stay here.' A flippant comment about whether he would be denied entry to this building too crossed his mind. He dismissed it as childish – the man was just doing his job and following the orders of the senior officer at the scene.

The constable, a man called Dobbs, had been about to ask what the old man wanted. Showing up at two places of interest minutes apart wasn't exactly suspicious – it might have been if he'd shown his face and then turned around. However, there was something about the way the old man looked at him; a knowing look that suggested he knew more than Dobbs ever could.

This was down to Dobbs of course. He was inherently lazy and would much rather drink in the pub while watching football than study for his sergeant's exam which was why he'd failed it four times already. He hadn't bothered to sit it at all this year.

Every member of his training group had already been promoted. He joked about it but secretly harboured a grudge because the exam was too hard – people shouldn't have to study for hours and hours once they left school. All in all, he had quite a chip on his shoulder and disliked anyone who he believed might attempt to get the upper hand.

'You'll have to wait here, sir,' he commanded. 'I'll need to check to see if guests are permitted to enter at this time.'

Albert found he was biting his upper lip. The man was just standing there, physically blocking the way into the hotel but having claimed he would need to check with a superior, he was making no attempt to do so. Biting his lip was Albert's unconscious habit when he wanted to tear a strip off someone and paused to debate whether he should.

Continuing to advance until he was almost within touching distance of the dull-looking constable, Albert chose a different option.

'Hello?' he shouted. His call was aimed not at the man standing three feet away, but at a woman just inside the doors talking to another officer.

Her head twitched around to see who was shouting.

'Sir I have told you that you need to wait. There is a murder investigation underway.'

Albert could not control the frown that formed.

'A murder investigation?'

'That's right, sir. There are plenty of establishments you can retire to for an hour or more. If you do not remove yourself from this vicinity, I will escort you elsewhere.'

Albert scoffed, 'And abandon your post?'

The hotel door opened before Dobbs could reply, the lady in plain clothes leaning out with a grimace at the drizzle wetting her hair.

'Can I help you, sir?'

Dobbs started to say something, but Albert cut right over the top of him.

'I'm a resident here. Is there any reason why I cannot come in?'

The woman – Albert's eye could pick her out as a senior detective from a mile away – frowned as if confused why he would ask.

'No.'

'Ah, jolly good,' Albert cheered. As the constable's face reddened and he looked straight ahead so his boss couldn't see it, Albert added, 'Your constable is telling passers-by that there has been a murder. You may wish to re-educate him on a few policies.'

The woman rolled her eyes. 'Dobbs you and I are going to have a conversation shortly that you will not enjoy.' Her expression was hard and her lips tight when she growled at the back of the constable's head. Softening her face, she pushed the door fully open and stepped out into the rain to hold it. 'Please,' she encouraged.

Albert kept his eyes pointed ahead, dismissing the ridiculous constable without a glance in his direction.

Keen to get inside, now he could see that was what they were doing, Rex lunged for the door. He wasn't a fan of the rain at the best of times.

Albert knew the dog well enough to anticipate the move, leaning backward to counter Rex's thrust, he still found himself jerked forward. He stumbled, losing his footing to collide with the lady holding the door.

'Sorry!' Albert spat the word as he yanked on the lead to bring his headstrong dog under control.

Rex was inside now, his feet on the rough mat designed to take the dirt off shoes, and that was all he needed to achieve. Checking over his shoulder, he found his human wrestling a woman. He understood mating, but human interactions were beyond his ability to decipher.

A swift fumbling of limbs got Albert back upright without him touching any parts of the lady where his hands ought not to go.

'Are you all right?' the lady asked once she was sure the old man was steady again.

Rippling his lips with an embarrassed huff of breath, Albert eyed his dog, 'Perfectly fine, thank you. Wanted to get inside did you, Rex?' he posed a rhetorical question and got a tail wag in response.

Seizing the opportunity, since he was already talking to the female detective, Albert asked, 'Since I already know you have a murder investigation on your hands, can I ask who it is?' Quickly raising a hand to stave off her response, he swiftly added, 'I know you are about to deliver the official line about not releasing information, but the victim is a resident here so I will find out soon enough anyway.'

The detective hitched one eyebrow, studying the old man. He had a curious way of asking questions.

'No, sir. I am not at liberty to provide any information at this time.'

He nodded in acceptance. Her answer was the one he expected.

At his feet, Rex was sniffing the air and looking around. The hotel smelled of food. There were biscuits in a nearby room, and tea – Earl Grey if he was not mistaken. The biscuits were rich tea, and as he attuned his hearing, he thought he heard a person crunch one.

He licked his lips, an unconscious reaction.

Albert thanked the detective, nodded to the uniformed sergeant still waiting patiently for him to move on, and walked to the reception desk.

A lady appeared there. She was in her fifties and professionally attired in a suit with a colourful cravat filling the gap between her collars. Flawlessly made up, she greeted him with a smile and would have asked his name had he not announced himself first.

'Good afternoon. I'm Albert Smith. I have a two-night reservation in one of your suites. Can you tell me who was murdered?' His question was a chance gambit posed because he had stayed in enough small hotels and B&Bs to know how often the receptionists craved conversation and the opportunity to gossip.

'Ooh, yes,' she beamed, forgetting the computer screen and her need to check his reservation. 'It was that Chris Caan off the telly, the famous chef. They say he was poisoned.'

Behind him, the detective tutted loudly. Albert half turned so he could meet her eyes and mouthed a quick, 'Sorry.' That the dead man was Chris Caan came as a surprise. The town was full of people visiting to attend his live event. His untimely demise was going to ruin a lot of plans.

Fixing his gaze on the receptionist again, he nodded thoughtfully. 'Poisoned, eh? An ironic way for a chef to go.' Albert leaned forward, getting closer so he could speak in a conspiratorial manner. In case there could be any ambiguity in his actions, he risked a cheeky glance back across the lobby to the two cops now watching him. 'Who do you think did it?'

The receptionist shot her own eyes at the cops just inside the hotel's front doors, a smile teasing her lips. 'I haven't the foggiest, but I dare say there will be a whole list of suspects.'

Her reply cued up a fresh barrage of questions, but the elevator pinged to Albert's left and a woman burst from it.

She was looking at the reception desk until she spotted the uniformed officer. She had a phone gripped tightly in her hand, a panicked look on her face, and tears brimming in her eyes.

'Is it true?' she blurted, a sob escaping with the words. 'Is he dead?'

The lady was in her late twenties or possibly just over the thirty mark. She was attractive, in an understated way, which is to say quite attractive but almost devoid of makeup, clad in functional clothing, and wearing her hair – a deep, natural auburn shade – tied back into a simple ponytail. Albert noted her height, after quickly checking her feet to see if she wore heels (she didn't), at five feet nine inches. Her figure was willowy, and she had bright green eyes that burst from her face against the auburn hair and a smattering of freckles left over from her youth.

The police officers exchanged a look. Albert realised what was happening now just from the look on their faces. They were here to deliver notice of death - to the widow, he assumed. He doubted the woman now waiting for an answer was the TV chef's wife, but he could be mistaken. Chris Caan had to be well into his fifties, but people married out of their age group all the time and his fame must have brought money which was attractive enough for some people. He didn't judge.

The problem the cops faced, was they needed to break the news and then start rifling through the victim's belongings; every second counted in a murder investigation. Albert knew this only too well.

They were waiting for something. Maybe for the wife to come to them, or perhaps they were waiting for her to return to the hotel. Albert couldn't guess, but now they faced a dilemma because word was already spreading.

Having received no answer to her question in the two seconds that followed it, the red head held up her phone.

'It's right here!' she screeched. 'It's all over social media! There are pictures of his dead body lying on the floor and then of a body bag going into a coroner's van!'

The female detective swore quietly, baring her teeth as she glared at the floor. Chris Caan collapsed in a crowded restaurant, of course there were pictures on the internet. The first responders cleared the restaurant but that was minutes after he fell ill. He was already dead by the time the police arrived. After sucking in a quick breath to compose herself, she met the red head's eyes with a neutral expression.

'Can you come with me, please? This is not a matter I can discuss in public.'

The red head froze, a choked gasp of horror jolting her whole body.

'Oh, my goodness! It is true!' She then chose to dissolve.

Rex watched the interplay from his spot on the carpet. If he understood things correctly, someone had been murdered. He'd learned that word during police training though the concept still eluded him. Humans seemed ready to kill each other at the slightest provocation. Often for almost no reason. He figured it was a territory thing; one human crossing a boundary that as a dog he was unable to perceive. Or it was to do with mating which always complicated matters.

Mostly, he was thinking his human needed something to distract him so that Rex could investigate the biscuits he could still smell. The latest scent was coming from behind the reception desk. What he couldn't see or smell was the small room to the right of reception as one looked at it.

The lady behind the desk, who was now watching proceedings intently, had forgotten her cup of tea and half eaten two-pack of jammy dodgers.

Unable to stop himself, Albert went to the red head as her face crumpled in on itself and she began to wilt and fold. It was a masculine trait that bordered on chauvinism, but his need to go to the aid of a woman in distress was wired in deep and would never be shifted.

Carefully placing an arm around her shoulder, he let Rex's lead go. Catching the dog's eyes, he said, 'Stay, Rex.'

Rex gave a wag of his tail. The old man wanted him to stay, and Rex would absolutely do that. Although, if he was being honest, Rex believed that instruction allowed for some artistic interpretation.

'Let's find you a seat, shall we?' Albert suggested, attempting to steer the red head away from the lobby. He shot his eyes at the lady behind the reception desk, imploring her to help him. 'Is there somewhere private we can go?'

In Albert's opinion, the cops should have reacted faster, and they should have been able to anticipate this happening. At seventy-eight, Albert had little use for, nor interest in, social media, yet he knew it was everywhere. Everyone had a phone and could livestream – another word he learned recently – from anywhere. That someone had taken pictures of Chris Caan's body should come as no surprise.

The receptionist hurried along behind the desk to a door at the end, spotted her cup of tea, and biscuits, gave them a longing look, and accepted she would need to make a new one. Muttering inside her head that never finding time to eat was why she stayed so thin, she pointed to a door on the other side of the lobby.

Albert flicked his eyes to the cops, the female detective and the man in uniform were being swept up in his decision to manage the situation. They followed obediently, going around Albert to get to the door just as the lady from reception opened it.

They filed inside, Albert guiding the red head with a hand on her shoulder.

'Can you watch my dog?' he whispered to the reception lady as he passed her. 'He should be no bother. I'll be out in a few seconds.'

The red head was sobbing still. 'I can't believe he's gone. He was such a lovely man.'

Unsure what her relationship to the deceased might be, he asked, 'Can you tell me your name? I'm Albert Smith.'

'Rachel Grainger. I'm Chris's producer. We've been working together for years.'

'We can take it from here, sir.'

Albert heard the detective speak but chose to ignore her much the same way he would have one of his subordinates many years ago. His focus was on the grieving lady to his front. When he was content Rachel was sitting comfortably and had been able to blow her nose on the clean handkerchief he kept in his left breast pocket specifically for such occasions, he came out of his kneeling crouch.

Stepping back to give the officers access, he said, 'All yours.' They expected him to leave, so it came as no surprise when the uniformed sergeant, a man with a trim black beard, invited him to do just that.

'No!' cried Rachel. 'I want him to stay.' Tear-filled eyes met Albert's and she asked him, 'If that's okay.'

Albert gave her a nod and a tight smile.

For the detective, it was better if the red head had someone with her. Delivery notice of death was never fun, but always worse when there was no one with the bereaved to help them, or share their grief.

Outside the door, Albert could hear the beginnings of a ruckus. A man's voice was raised and though muffled, it sounded agitated.

The detective started speaking, bringing Albert's focus back to the room.

'Rachel, my name is Detective Inspector Brownlow.' The detective introduced herself and delivered the awful news. She was sympathetic and did a good job in Albert's opinion. She would, of course, have to do it again because Rachel was not the next of kin. Rachel's appearance and unexpected display of emotions had changed the officers' plans, but it wasn't like they could refuse to confirm it when the woman had pictures on her phone.

'How did he die?' Rachel wanted to know. 'Was it poison? That's what they are saying on the web. He ate something and keeled over instantly. What was he doing back at Parsons' Hotpot Place?'

DI Brownlow said, 'Our investigation is ongoing.'

It was a standard cop response that gave a reply without providing any information.

Rachel didn't seem to need an answer though. 'He was, wasn't he? It was that bitch wife of his. I don't know how, but you can bet your life on it. She's got a huge life insurance policy out on him. He wants to leave her, but the fool made her his partner when they first got married. It was a tax thing; they saved some money if his income was shared. But now it just means he is trapped.'

Albert's detective brain wanted to know why the TV star would reveal such intimate information to his producer; a woman half his age. However, that wasn't the only thing triggering a spark in his head. There was the small matter that Rachel claimed the death was by poisoning. Chris Caan keeled over in the hotpot place so surely it should be the people working there who were under suspicion.

Unable to stop himself, he asked, 'Was Mrs Caan at the restaurant?'

Both cops and Rachel swung their heads to look at him, but their expressions were very different. It was clear that Rachel didn't know the answer – her face was a blank. The cops though, were unhappy that he was speaking. It was not his place to ask questions, though they would not be so impolite as to point that out.

Not yet.

'She was not,' replied the detective inspector before adding, 'Mr Smith no further questions, please.'

Albert mimed zipping his lips shut and turned his attention back to Rachel, wondering what more she might have to say.

The cops stayed quiet too, listening because they had a person spilling information that might prove pertinent to the case without them needing to interview her. Only when Rachel stopped talking, did DI Brownlow start.

'You believe Mrs Caan wished her husband harm? Do you have any evidence?'

Strangely, just as Albert thought Rachel was going to say something key, she chose to divert the conversation.

'Um, I think I should call my husband,' she said, deflecting the question. 'I need to call the station manager too; he will need to know.' She put a hand to her head as she lifted her phone once more. 'Oh, goodness, I need to tell the whole crew. We are still filming the series,' she explained. 'At least we were supposed to be.'

DI Brownlow stopped her. 'Mrs Grainger. I must insist you let us speak to Mrs Caan first. My duty is to deliver the notice of death to the immediate next of kin.'

Albert was sure DI Brownlow would start out with that. Then, once the tears were dwindling, the detective would start with some hard questions. The slip up from Rachel, if that was what it was, would be front and centre in the detective inspector's mind. Charged with catching a killer, she would look for a swift resolution.

Not only that, the loved one was often the killer. Too often, in fact.

The noise from outside was getting louder. Loud enough that it was getting difficult to ignore.

'Is she in here?' demanded a voice from the other side of the door. It got an answer, but the other speaker, the reception lady, Albert guessed, was speaking at a normal volume so her words went unheard. 'I don't care who's in there!' the man snapped, and the door opened inward.

The uniformed officer had already moved to intercept.

'Sir, please adjust your temperament,' the bearded sergeant suggested in a voice that held an unwavering edge.

The man outside had a completely bald head. He was in his thirties, with blue eyes and tanned skin from a sunbed. As the door swung wider, Albert could see the man was a shade over six feet tall and lifted weights regularly though not professionally. He was looking around and past the cop blocking his entry, trying to find something inside the room.

'Rachel,' he shouted. 'Upset, are you? There's a surprise.' He was mocking her grief. In Albert's opinion, he deserved a jolly good punch on the nose. He also noticed that Rex wasn't where he left him.

Incompetent Constable

Rex was behind the reception counter. He'd been patient, waiting for the right opportunity, rather than go too soon and risk tipping his hand. When the humans crossed the lobby to go into a room, he thought he was going to be left completely alone. Had that been the case, he would have acted immediately.

The lady from behind the desk returned though. He got a pat on the head and a chin scratch, which was all very pleasant, but those biscuits were not going to eat themselves. It was only when a new man arrived, the upset woman's mate, he surmised with one sniff, that his chance came.

The man caused a distraction and, once no one was looking, rather than wait for the perfect opportunity only for it to never occur, he let himself through the door to get behind reception and there he claimed his prize.

One biscuit was mostly gone, but the other was still in its little cellophane packet. Had he been in a hurry, the wrapper would have gotten eaten too, yet he preferred to take the few seconds required to carefully extract it.

His great size made swooping on treats humans left above dog head height easy. Not only that, he thought to himself as he jumped up to place his paws either side of the mug of tea, humans made fun drinks and being tall meant he could get to them.

The man was being good enough to ensure the distraction he created was a loud one so no one heard the hurried liquid lapping sound as Rex dredged the bottom of the tea mug.

Less than five yards away, and perfectly aware that if his dog wasn't in sight, the sneaky git was probably trying to find food, Albert nevertheless didn't feel that he could extricate himself to go looking for Rex at this time. Mostly that was because the newcomer, clearly Rachel's husband or boyfriend, was blocking the door and causing unnecessary distress.

Rachel, still tearful, got to her feet. 'I've told you a dozen times, Jasper, I was not having an affair with Chris.'

The man sneered, 'At least a dozen. He's dead then, is he?'

DI Brownlow rolled her eyes again and sighed. 'Oh, for goodness sake. Sergeant Pike please bring the gentleman inside and close the door.'

Albert started toward the door. 'I need to check the whereabouts of my dog. He is prone to wander.'

'One moment, please, Mr Smith.'

Albert turned his head to look back at the detective inspector but didn't stop walking.

'Please?' she implored. 'I will not take up more than a few seconds.'

Sergeant Pike had the bald man inside the room and the door closed before Albert could get to it. He felt that was a little unfair but chose to remain silent so the DI could speak – it seemed the swiftest method of escape.

'I need to speak with Mrs Caan. I have to deliver the news of her husband's death and I need, therefore, to keep any of you from speaking to her first.'

Albert let a frown form. 'Why were you waiting in reception? Surely, if Mrs Caan isn't here you should be going through her room. This is a murder investigation as I understand it. Or do you already have the killer in custody?'

'You won't need to look far for the killer,' scoffed Jasper. 'I should expect his wife did it. Probably because he has been shagging my wife.' He was looking at Rachel when he delivered the claim, cruelly twisting the verbal knife.

Rachel blew her top. 'Arrrrhh! For the last time, Jasper. If you really think I was having sex with that old man, why haven't you left me? Why are we still together?'

Jasper fixed her with hard eyes and growled his response. 'Till death do us part, love.'

Detective Inspector Sarah Brownlow was not used to having this much drama all piled one problem on top of another. Jasper Grainger – she correctly assumed the husband and wife shared the last name – was the second person to accuse the victim's wife. She tried to keep an open mind, but also silently acknowledged that it would be a nice, neat solution if Mrs Caan were behind her husband's death, and they could find evidence to secure a quick confession.

Frowning at Albert, who still waited for his question to be answered, she had to admit she wasn't used to being quizzed by members of the public; that was a task for those above her paygrade. The old man was either well informed, or a former serving police officer. She thought the latter to be more likely, and then a worrying thought occurred to her. She would have to check, but there was talk … rumour might be a better term, of an old man and his dog solving crimes.

There was a bulletin this morning that she didn't get time to read. It was about a drugs bust in Dundee where a huge pack of dogs had caused havoc for the police tactical unit. There had been other reports though,

24

the same easy-to-ignore description of an old man and a dog cropping up in different parts of the country. Could this be the same man?

Sarah Brownlow – on the fast track to the top of the tree – did not want some random civilian solving her cases. Most especially not one that was going to hit the news headlines in a few hours.

Drawing her thoughts back to the room, the couple were bickering now. Standing almost toe to toe, it was beginning to look like Rachel was going to be the one to get physical. Her hands were clenching into fists, her body language that of someone who has been pushed too far.

Before the marital spat could descend any further, DI Brownlow raised her voice.

'That's enough! Both of you simmer down. I will be taking statements later and I will expect fact, not conjecture.' She watched the husband and wife to make sure they were going to comply, then shifted her gaze back to Albert. 'Sir, even if I had a suspect in custody, I would not be able to tell you about it. As for why you found us waiting in reception – the receptionist discovered the spare key to Mr and Mrs Caan's suite was missing. She had to call her supervisor to bring a master key. We are still waiting for that person to arrive.'

Albert was surprised to hear they still used actual keys at this hotel. He much preferred them; little slips of plastic were not to be trusted. However, the missing key sounded suspicious.

From outside the door came a shriek.

'What now?' sighed DI Brownlow, nodding her head to Sergeant Pike. He opened the door again.

All he needed was a glimpse through a crack in the door. He pulled his head back inside and whispered, 'It's Mrs Caan.' He glanced her way again, then threw the door open, and started running.

Lying on the carpet in front of the reception desk was a woman in an elegant winter coat. She'd fainted, Albert surmised. Trained by decades of work, his eyes needed just a split second to take in her body shape, hair colour, shoes, and other factors. Even though lying down and scrunched a little, Albert estimated her height at an average five feet and seven inches and her age to be mid-fifties. She was a blonde, but not naturally so. Her clothes were expensive, as one might expect given her husband's celebrity status, and at a hundred and twenty pounds – Albert's rough guess – she was both slender and attractive.

He also noted that Rex was back in position where Albert had told him to stay a couple of minutes ago.

Rex wagged his tail. His human was approaching. He liked the old man; they went lots of fun places and there were often things to eat or people to chase. He didn't exactly have a place to call home – the concept that this was a trip with a finite duration was beyond his ability to understand, but his human kept his water bowl and his doggy chow with him, so Rex didn't mind too much.

The new woman had walked in just as he was settling on the carpet for a snooze. He'd eaten the biscuits and drunk the tea, then looked about to see if there was anything else he could find. Accepting there wasn't, he went back to the spot where his human wanted him to stay.

So far as he was concerned, he'd pulled off a brilliant sneak. Even if the humans noticed the tea and biscuits were gone, they wouldn't think to blame him – he hadn't moved.

Satisfied he was beyond suspicion, he sniffed the air. His human was coming, other people rushing to get there first including the man in police uniform. As a former police dog, fired for having poor attitude, he looked upon police officers as good guys.

Until he learned otherwise, that is.

Sucking in a deep noseful of the lady's scent, Rex noted her perfume – it was distinct from anything the other humans were wearing and bore a heavy tangerine note accented with jasmine blossom. It would be easy to recall should he need to ever. Rex knew to check for overlaid scents, those that had rubbed off onto the lady as she touched or came close to other humans.

He sniffed again to be sure, but he detected nothing on her that he'd also found on other humans in the last half an hour since they left the bus. She did smell of the hotpot though. He checked his memory, questioning if it was the same blend of herbs he smelled at the restaurant they couldn't get into.

Before he could confirm it, he detected something else. It was a sort of medicinal smell. He sniffed again, using his eyes as well for once as he looked about. The woman's handbag had spilled its contents when she fell; keys, phone, and other detritus littering the floor in a small radius by her right hand.

Among the items was a small prescription pill bottle. Rex couldn't read the label of course, but he got to his feet and nudged it with a paw. Sniffing deeply with his nose a half inch from the bottle cap, he analysed the smell. It was not one he recognised.

Albert watched as the two police officers knelt either side of the stricken woman. Sergeant Pike had to wave his arm at Rex so he would back up a little and make room.

The lady was breathing and had a steady pulse, the cops reported to each other.

DI Brownlow looked up at the two women wearing suits in hotel colours. They had rushed around from behind the reception desk and were looking very sheepish.

The new woman had bright red cheeks. 'Sorry,' she blushed. 'I didn't know who it was,' she explained.

'What happened?' asked Brownlow as she got to her feet. 'Who are you, please?'

'I'm Debra Kerr. I'm the assistant manager.' Her scarlet cheeks deepened another shade.

'I'm Sue Beckett,' volunteered the lady from reception even though or possibly because no one had asked.

She got ignored by everyone because her manager was speaking again.

'I was asking Sue where the officers had gone and this lady came into reception,' she indicated the unconscious form on the carpet. Sergeant Pike was holding her right hand and trying to coax her back to life. 'She overheard what I was saying.'

DI Brownlow let her head fall forward and closed her eyes – she knew what was coming.

Still scarlet, Debra admitted, 'Well, long story short, she asked why the police were here and I told her. I didn't know who she was,' Debra protested again.

The senior detective had a rage-filled mask for a face, but it wasn't aimed at the assistant manager. Huffing with exasperation, she twisted her body to look back out through the glass panels of the hotel front doors. Albert tracked her eyes to see the same thing.

Constable Dobbs wasn't at his post.

DI Brownlow sucked in a deep breath to power her angry shout. 'Dobbs! Dobbs, you cretin! Get in here!'

Wide eyed and moving fast – as if reacting now would make any difference – Constable Dobbs appeared from around the corner and burst through the doors. Unfortunately, in his haste he snagged his sleeve, and running forward found his motion abruptly arrested.

His feet left the floor, causing an out of place comedy moment where he hung in the air for a split second, shock and question ruling his face before he crashed back to the carpet.

DI Brownlow sighed and hung her head, her exasperated breath loud enough for everyone to hear.

While Dobbs scrambled to get back on his feet, she demanded to know, 'What was the task you were primarily stationed at the door to do, Dobbs?'

Looking as though he thought it might be a trick question, he replied, but with a lack of certainty.

'To identify and intercept Mrs Caan when she returned, Ma'am?' He posed it as a question.

'And yet, I find her in a faint on the lobby carpet having mysteriously entered the building without being stopped. Did she pull a Jedi mind trick on you? Hmmm? Or did an interestingly shaped cloud catch your attention thus allowing Mrs Caan to slip by without you noticing?'

Albert felt the detective inspector was overstepping on the public humiliation but had to question just how far Constable Dobbs had pushed her patience so far today.

The junior officer seemed confused by the question. Mrs Caan was coming around when he said, 'I was overdue a smoke break, Ma'am. I didn't want to bother you with it, so I just ...' His voice trailed off as the detective inspector's glare burned into him.

He got ignored as Sergeant Pike helped Mrs Caan to sit up and DI Brownlow came into a crouch so their heads were the same height.

'Mrs Caan, my name is Detective Inspector Brownlow ...'

Albert wanted to get checked in, put his bags in his room, and maybe go for a pint somewhere. He had been travelling for a good portion of the day and though he'd been sitting for most of it, the seats on the trains were not the most comfortable. A cold glass of ale and a snack of some kind would tide him over until dinner in a few hours.

Unfortunately, with the drama unravelling right in front of the hotel's reception desk, Albert had no choice but to wait.

Rachel and Jasper were waiting too. The husband and wife were not seeking comfort by holding each other as one might expect of a married couple. Was there something to Jasper's claim? His belief that his wife had been having an affair sounded unshakeable. Rachel's denial had been equally convincing. However, they both agreed the wife would be the most likely suspect for her husband's murder.

Albert watched as DI Brownlow attempted to do her duty and officially deliver her terrible news. A hotel lobby is not the place to do it, but Mrs Caan demanded to know the truth the moment she was conscious again.

The news caused her to swoon a second time, though only momentarily. She burst into racking sobs, tears flowing as she denied it could be true.

Albert half expected Rachel or Jasper to say something cutting. Their opinion earlier was that Mrs Caan had no love for her husband, yet the display of grief Albert bore witness to would be hard to fake.

It took more than a minute to get the grief-stricken woman, the second one since Albert walked through the hotel doors with Rex, moving again. A nod from DI Brownlow signalled that Debra the assistant manager should get the elevator – they were taking Mrs Caan up to her room.

Finally alone when the elevator door closed, Albert breathed a silent sigh of relief. Whatever was going on here was none of his concern and he would happily pay it no mind. He was going to enjoy the hotpot and go on his merry way.

However, stepping up to the reception desk, his brow furrowed. Would the hotpot shop be open again in the next day or so? If Chris Caan had died on the premises, how long would it stay shut? There were other places he could get the dish, but he came to Clitheroe for the one voted the best.

So lost in thought was he that he missed what Sue the receptionist said to him.

'I'm sorry,' he gave the lady his full attention.

'Oh, nothing, dear. Let's get you checked in, shall we? I was just musing on what might have happened to my tea and biscuits.'

Rex made sure to look away, studying the wall on the opposite side of the lobby. Had he been able to, he might have whistled a tune to show how innocent he must be.

Albert and Rex could both hear the argument before the elevator doors opened on their floor. They were at the top of the hotel in one of the suites. Much of the rest of the top floor was booked out to the TV crew, according to Sue. Albert had a good gossip with her once the police officers and all the drama in the lobby cleared out.

Sue happily revealed how big a draw Chris Caan proved to be. According to her the town had been advertising his visit for months. If her report was accurate, most of the visitors in town were here for the live baking event tonight.

There will be a lot of disappointed people, Albert thought darkly as he stepped out of the enclosed box and onto the carpeted hallway of the hotel's top floor.

'What on earth do you mean? You're not letting us leave? Do you think we could have had anything to do with Chris's death?'

The person raising their voice was Rachel Grainger. Her tears were gone but her eyes were puffy and red, and her makeup ruined.

Unable to help himself, Albert listened in.

Rex sniffed. There was a trace of the hotpot in the air again, bay and just a touch of nutmeg, tonal flavours added to give richness and depth. The dog couldn't know it, but what he was able to smell were two of the secret ingredients that ensured the hotpot won more than half the awards and competitions Danny Parsons entered. No one knew the secret recipe, not even Danny's family members who worked in the restaurant with him every day.

Rivals would have given anything to be able to know what the dog had just perceived in a single sniff. That he could smell it came as no surprise. Half the people he'd met so far stank of it.

'Mrs Grainger ...' DI Brownlow started to explain, only to be interrupted instantly.

Rachel scoffed, 'Not for long.'

DI Brownlow ignored the remark. 'Mrs Grainger until I have established the facts and recorded statements from all members of Mr Caan's party, I must insist that you remain in Clitheroe. You are booked in for another night, are you not?' DI Brownlow asked the question in a way that told Albert she already knew the answer.

'Yes, but I don't see,' this time it was Rachel's turn to have her words spoken over.

'You were happy to point the finger at Mrs Caan earlier, Mrs Grainger. I have questions that you will need to answer. Your husband too.'

'Is that right?' asked Mrs Caan, coming into the hallway from her room with an abrupt suddenness. Her door had appeared closed a moment earlier, but DI Brownlow's proximity suggested she might have only just left it, perhaps stepping outside to intercept Rachel.

Moving to get a better view, Albert spotted a suitcase behind Mrs Grainger. She had been trying to leave.

Mrs Caan's face was even more red and blotchy than Rachel's, her tears still falling. But the overpowering sadness she felt was fighting for dominance now with a show of anger directed at the younger woman.

'You accused me, did you?' she snarled through her grief. 'You think I would want my husband dead?'

Rachel's cheeks flushed deep red, but she shook her head to clear it and levelled a direct accusation instead of backing down.

'Yes, Emelia, I think you did want him dead. I think you have wanted him dead for some time. He knew about the life insurance policy, you know.'

'Whisper that in your ear, did he? You think I don't know you were sleeping with him?'

Rachel threw her arms in the air. 'There it is again. Why does everyone think I was sleeping with Chris? How about if the detective inspector here asks you why you felt a need to take out such a large insurance policy six months before he died, huh? Why don't we do that?'

Albert could tell the DI wanted to know precisely that but hadn't gotten around to posing the question herself yet. She was listening keenly for Emelia Caan's response.

'It hardly matters what I did,' snarled Emelia. 'Chris was poisoned in the hotpot place. I haven't even been there, and it will not be difficult to establish my alibi. I was at a spa getting a massage and have a dozen witnesses. Can you account for your whereabouts, Rachel?'

Rachel reacted as if slapped and lunged for her opponent.

DI Brownlow was swift to step into her path.

'That's enough. Both of you,' she growled.

Sergeant Pike appeared, also leaving Mrs Caan's room where he had undoubtedly remained expecting the bereaved wife and his boss to return.

'I don't need an alibi,' snapped Rachel, all but spitting in Mrs Caan's face. 'None of us do. I don't know how you did it yet, but you are to blame for the poisonous hotpot he was fed.'

'The hotpot was not poisonous,' DI Brownlow's comment stopped the two women dead.

Albert put down his suitcase and slipped the backpack off his shoulders; this was getting good.

Mrs Caan squinted, her face pinched as she questioned what she was hearing.

'You told me Chris ate the hotpot and became ill within a few seconds. He then lost consciousness and never regained it. You told me that,' she insisted, her eyes locked on Brownlow's.

The detective spared a glance at her sergeant, imploring eyes asking for help she wasn't going to get. Albert knew well enough that the boss must be able to stand alone and fend for themselves.

Accepting that she needed to provide an explanation, Brownlow said, 'The proprietor proved there was nothing wrong with his hotpot by eating some right in front of me. Nothing happened to him. That is why none of you are leaving town. Chris Caan was poisoned, but it wasn't as simple as it was made to look.' It was a carefully worded accusation. So far as the detective inspector was concerned, Chris Caan's death was suspicious. It was not quite the same as labelling this a murder enquiry; the cause of his death was yet to be established, yet she clearly believed there was reason for her to investigate.

And the people she would be investigating were the ones closest to the deceased.

Along the corridor, a small ray of hope swelled. If the hotpot wasn't to blame, maybe the restaurant would reopen. Albert chose to be optimistic.

Rex wasn't thinking about that. He was questioning something he heard Mrs Caan say. He needed to get closer to be certain because she claimed to have not been to the hotpot place. The scent of it was on her. Rex needed to get close enough to have a really good sniff, but the trace of it he got in the lobby before other things distracted him, left him with little doubt he was right.

Rex tended to trust his nose, it rarely steered him wrong and was much more reliable than eyesight or hearing. He liked solving mysteries. That his police handlers never listened to him when he solved crimes before they were even up to speed with the clues had been a constant source of frustration.

Ultimately, it had been that, and his dwindling tolerance for the humans' stupidity that led to his expulsion from the canine police service.

The old man he was with now was much better and had learned to listen. Rex chose to stay quiet for now. He would keep on sniffing and help out later if there was a chance to.

The two ladies, Emelia Caan and Rachel Grainger, had momentarily forgotten to bicker with each other. Their combined attention was solely on DI Brownlow.

'How can he be poisoned by something that isn't poisonous?' Rachel wanted to know.

Emelia asked, 'Did you try it? Maybe the proprietor took an antidote or something beforehand so he could eat it?'

Rachel screwed up her face. 'That would mean the proprietor of the hotpot place is the killer. Why would some random restaurant owner want to kill Chris? Chris was putting the hotpot place on the map by filming an episode of his new TV show there. Danny Parsons was nothing but grateful I can assure you. You're just trying to cover your own tracks,' she accused.

Emelia's question was yet to be answered, but she no longer cared. Accused again, she was drawing back her lips to scream something at Rachel.

DI Brownlow jumped in to stop her. 'The two of you need to ceasefire. Accusing each other will resolve nothing.' Her voice was hard and commanding and got a nod of approval from Albert. She made eye contact with both women before speaking again. 'No, I did not taste it and would have stopped Mr Parsons from doing so too had I been able to get to him quickly enough. The hotpot was secured for analysis. The staff at Parsons' Perfect Hotpots will be interviewed, but they are not suspects at this time.'

'But we are?' snapped Mrs Caan, fuelled with indignation.

DI Brownlow almost smiled at the unintended cue. 'Tell me about the insurance policy you have on your husband, Mrs Caan.'

It was a red rag to a bull.

'How dare you?' Mrs Caan shrieked. 'How dare you suggest I could have any involvement. I shall be speaking with your superiors. I have never been so insulted!' There were more words to come but she couldn't get them out. The pain of her husband's passing returned in the midst of her rage, stealing her breath as fresh tears began to fall.

In a flurry of movement, she spun around and ran back into her hotel suite.

DI Brownlow had been clumsy in Albert's opinion. It was something he had been guilty of many times in his career. When they were emotional was often the best time to question people. They were rarely thinking straight, their guard wasn't up, and so one could glean information or details they might otherwise do their best to hide.

It hadn't worked today; the wound was too fresh. Or Mrs Caan, if she was in any way guilty of having a hand in her husband's demise, was using the suddenness of her husband's passing to cover her tracks.

Either way, DI Brownlow would get nothing further in the immediate future.

A few seconds of silence followed Mrs Caan's departure, the people in the corridor each dwelling on their own thoughts until Rachel spoke.

'I need to be somewhere else. I cannot remain in my room with my husband and if you are going to insist I must, you are going to have to arrest me.' It was a challenge; the gauntlet was thrown down.

DI Brownlow was not going to be intimidated though.

'Mrs Grainger, you may move to a different room, or you may move hotel if you are able to find accommodation elsewhere. I understand there are very few rooms to be had anywhere in Clitheroe. Make sure you are contactable by phone and advise one of my officers where you do choose to reside.'

The detective inspector held her gaze for several seconds, challenging Rachel to make another bold statement. When none came, she chose to excuse herself.

'If you don't mind, I have an investigation to conduct.' DI Brownlow was about to duck back into the Caans' suite and Albert had to move fast to intercept her.

'DI Brownlow,' he called to get her attention.

Rex jumped back to his feet as his human rushed forward. Were they going into the lady's room? He would be able to get a proper sniff if they did.

DI Brownlow paused halfway through the door to see what the old man wanted. He'd listened in like a creepy stalker the whole time they were in the hallway. She'd wanted to tell him to move along but suspected he would only recite his right to be there and question her request until she backed down.

'Is there something you need, Mr Smith?' she made no attempt to hide the impatience she felt.

'If the hotpot is not the source of the poison, will you be keeping the restaurant shut?' Albert knew it was a trivial matter, and that the DI's best course of action was to seal the building until she could establish what had happened. That didn't work with his plans though, so he was happily being a fly in her ointment.

'Yes, Mr Smith.' It was the response he expected. 'Until I can be certain what happened to Mr Caan, Parsons' Perfect Hotpots will remain shut.'

That would most likely mean at least forty-eight hours. After that, unless she could prove there was a justified reason to enforce the closure, the restaurant would have the right to claim compensation and the DI's bosses would never allow it.

Albert nodded, accepting things for how they were, even if they were not how he wanted them to be.

Beneath the humans, Rex tried to slip through the door, his nose leading. He stopped abruptly when the lady in the doorway shifted her leg to block his way.

DI Brownlow wasn't finished with Mrs Caan's room. She wanted to bring a forensic team in, but Mrs Caan's need for a place to grieve and the lack of hard evidence that might justify searching the widow's hotel room and possessions, dictated it would have to wait.

All DI Brownlow had was some hearsay to point her at Mrs Caan, and half of it came from a woman who might have been sleeping with the deceased and thus have ulterior motive to discredit the widow.

Albert looped a hand through Rex's collar, pulling him backward even as the dog tried hard to snort in the air beyond the door.

'I need to smell the room,' Rex complained, whining loudly.

'Get that dog out,' insisted Sergeant Pike unnecessarily.

Albert had many things he wanted to say, but his detective's brain was working overtime on the problem already and left too little of his mind available to consider a reply or parting remark.

There were things missing from the equation, and from where Albert metaphorically stood, DI Brownlow was going to find herself hampered by her need to consider the widow's emotional state. He had no such restrictions, and if Albert wanted the hotpot place to reopen before he was due to move on, he was going to have to make sure the police figured out who the real killer was.

41

Heading back along the hallway to his own suite, Albert grabbed his suitcase and backpack. There was a determined set to his jaw.

It was mystery solving time.

The missing room key disturbed Albert. It was all too much coincidence for him to accept. He also didn't believe Rachel Grainger when she denied her involvement with Chris Caan. He doubted the woman was involved in his death, but their affair could easily be a factor.

The curious element was the poisoning. Chris Caan ate something that appeared immediately to result in his death, yet the proprietor – he recalled overhearing the man's name: Danny Parsons – had then eaten the same dish to prove it was edible.

That was where Albert wanted to start. Yet the restaurant was closed and that presented him with an obstacle to overcome.

Normally, upon arrival anywhere, Albert would unpack and lay out his things, make sure Rex had water et cetera. Today, the only thing he did was attend to his dog's needs.

'Here you go, boy.' He used the wall for support as he lowered the bowl of water to the floor. His knees both clicked as he came back to upright.

Rex sniffed the water, checking whether it was just water, or had something more interesting in it, then slaked his thirst.

He was keen to get back out and sniff a few of the humans. There were interesting smells around, and some kind of mystery to solve. He knew that not just because of the things the humans were saying – he heard them say murder several times – but because of the way his human was acting.

Rex had learned to read the old man's behaviours. His human would become grumpy if he were overly tired or hungry. He would drag his feet if Rex insisted they took a route the old man disagreed with, and easiest to spot was how distracted he became when there was a mystery to investigate.

Rex figured a lot of that was to do with how poorly his nose worked. Like all humans, the old man's olfactory system was a near-pointless failure of a sense. Mercifully, he had learned to pay attention when Rex could smell the clues. That was why Rex was now at the door waiting to go out. They would need to work together as a team for surely his human was acting distracted now because he was planning to find out who the murderer was.

Behind him, Albert patted down his pockets to make sure he had all that he needed before leaving the room and checked his phone to make sure the battery wasn't about to go flat.

Task complete, he started for the door. Rex was there, nose pointing outward as he waited for it to open. The dog looked over one shoulder and gave an encouraging wag of his tail.

Albert pursed his lips. 'Not this time, Rex. I need to do this one alone.'

Rex raised one eyebrow. 'Huh?' His human was trying to coax him away from the door.

'Come on, Rex. Let's make you a comfy spot in the corner, shall we?'

Rex wagged his tail again, failure to understand ruling his brow. 'I thought we were going out? I need to smell the clues.'

'Not this time,' replied Albert, correctly interpreting his dog's expression for once. 'I have to go undercover, and I cannot take you with me for that.'

Another minute of coaxing resulted only in Rex planting his furry backside by the door, effectively blocking Albert's exit.

'I'm not moving until you say we are going together. We both know I am the better detective. If you go without me, you will just stumble around using your eyes and ears and probably get into trouble. So let's stop this silly nonsense, shall we? There isn't a thing you can do to get me to change my mind.'

Accepting defeat, Albert gave up using encouragement to get the dog to move. Twenty years ago, when he was stronger, he would have picked the stupid dog up and shifted him. Since that was no longer an option, he reached into his pocket and from it produced Rex's kryptonite.

Mesmerised by the pig's ear now dangling enticingly from his human's hand, Rex failed to notice the drool beginning to slip from one corner of his jowls.

Albert backed away, drawing the dog across the room as if the treat in his hand were attached to Rex's head by an invisible string.

When he dropped it, Rex sprang forward, diving on the pig's ear to ensure no one else could get to it first. That there were no competitors in the room made no difference to his approach – it was too precious to risk there being an unseen rival waiting to swoop.

With closed eyes, and the treat pinned between his front paws, Rex gnawed and chewed the glistening gelatinous morsel. He crunched the crunchy bits, savoured the juicy bits, but ultimately ate it in under four seconds.

The sound of the door closing and the lock turning caused Rex to snap his eyes open again. Staring in disbelief at the door, he sighed and lowered his rueful head to the carpet as he muttered, 'Well played, sir. Well played.'

Albert left the hotel via the main entrance without seeing another person. Constable Dobbs was no longer outside guarding the way in – not that he had proven to be effective at the task. Nor was there a crime scene van in sight as Albert imagined there might be. A squad car parked on the opposite side of the street was the only indication anything might be amiss.

Word was going to spread though. It had taken Rachel minutes to find out about Chris Caan's death. She said they had more filming to do, and a live event planned in the town square. Would they reveal why the event was cancelled? Or publish a generic statement?

Albert decided it made no difference to what he was going to do, but was curious to discover if Rachel, Chris Caan's producer if he understood things correctly, would continue to handle the situation or not.

Leaving the hotel behind, Albert retraced his steps. He was heading for the closed hotpot place but needed to make a stop on the way for he had a plan.

Serendipity had chosen to place two shops next to each other that Albert spotted on his way through town earlier. Ordinarily, he would never have need to purchase the items they sold. However, today Albert believed he could buy props that would get him into Parsons' Perfect Hotpots and access to some of the people who witnessed Chris Caan's death.

In the first shop, a stationers, he bought a clipboard with a cover and a bound A4 pad on which to make notes. At the till, he spotted ID tags on lanyards, the sort a person might put an official identification in. He took one of them too, adding an extra couple of pounds to his bill.

Next door, in a rundown looking shop selling tabards, aprons, school uniforms, and items of work wear for all manner of industries, he found a white coat. There were several on hangers, pressed and ready to be worn.

At the till, a tall man in his sixties with wide shoulders and bushy brown hair took the garment and began to fold it neatly.

Albert stopped him. 'I need to wear that actually,' he chuckled, playing the part of a person caught out by an error. 'I managed to leave the house without mine and it would not do to inspect a restaurant for food safety if I am not correctly dressed myself.'

The man behind the counter cocked a quizzical expression. 'You're on your way to Parsons'?'

Albert gave a small nod of his head. 'Word travels fast, I see. Yes. The proprietor, Danny,' Albert dropped the name casually, 'requested we attend as swiftly as possible. I'm afraid I cannot go into the specifics of the matter ...'

The shop assistant laughed. 'Chris Caan dropped dead after eating the hotpot, mister. That sort of news doesn't stay secret for long. I take it Danny wants you to prove the hotpot wasn't to blame.'

'Indeed,' admitted Albert, lying through his teeth, but convinced he was playing the role well.

Placing his wallet on the counter in preparedness to pay, Albert picked up the white coat.

'I can add your firm's logo to it for an extra fiver if you like,' the man pointed out.

Albert almost replied that there was no need, but in the spirit of looking the part, an official logo would be just the thing. Instead of turning down the man's well-timed sales effort, Albert nodded and handed the garment back.

'That would be super. Thank you.'

'I just need to print one off. It's an iron-on sticker. They come off in the wash eventually, but it will be good for a few months at least. What's the name of the organisation?'

Albert tried to hide his panic as the man waited patiently for an answer. The shop assistant was at the computer behind the counter, ready to type Albert's response into a search bar. Seconds ticked by while Albert racked his brain for an answer.

When Albert said nothing, the man looked up expectantly.

'The name of the organisation?' he repeated, a vague sense of doubt creeping into his eyes.

Albert blurted, 'The Food Health Governing Body,' the name coming to him like a lightning bolt sent from heaven. With the words out, Albert realised he'd been holding his breath and now needed to take a gulp of air.

'Here, are you all right?' asked the shop assistant, concern clouding his face.

Albert could see no way to explain his behaviour other than to concoct another lie.

'I'm getting forgetful,' he mumbled, making certain to sound both ashamed and upset. It was all he needed to say, and it touched on a subject the shop assistant was only too happy to avoid exploring further.

A simple internet search provided the logo and five minutes later, Albert was leaving the shop with his official-looking Food Standards Governing Body coat over his day clothes and a clipboard gripped firmly in his right hand. The plastic ID wallet on its lanyard had been tucked into the front of the jacket between the third and fourth buttons so only the picture poked out.

It was his library card in the holder. The slightest scrutiny would reveal his scam, but he was feeling confident as he approached the restaurant premises and willing to risk getting caught to see if there was something to learn.

Had he known the chain of events he was about to set in motion, Albert would have gone for a pint instead.

Should Have Been on Stage

In the hotel, disgruntled with his human's decision to leave him behind, Rex was staring at the door. The scent of the hotpot, the clue he wanted to explore was down to trace amounts now. He could barely smell it at all through the gap under the door.

His human was out there somewhere now looking for clues of his own – at least, that was Rex's belief, and it irked him that he had to sit on the bench when he was poised and ready to be on the pitch. That wasn't the analogy Rex used, obviously; he had no knowledge nor interest in human games. He thought about the current situation in terms of having teeth but being denied the chance to bite the problem.

It is a universal truth that dogs are always on the wrong side of a closed door, but hearing footsteps outside, Rex chose to do something about it.

Lying down with his nose pressed up against the small gap at the base of the door, he began to whine. He made it as plaintive and sad as he could muster. Loud too - he upped the volume to ensure he could be heard.

The footsteps, heading from left to right as they passed the door, paused a few yards later. Rex could tell it was a man; the mix of perspiration and cologne was unmistakable. Furthermore, he suspected it was a man he got a brief sniff of earlier – the one with no hair on his head.

To make sure the man outside got the message, Rex gave another pain-filled whine; high-pitched and woeful. Then he had to stop his tail from wagging when the footsteps turned around and came right back to his door.

'Hello?' the man's voice called through the door. 'Is there anyone in there? Is the dog okay?'

'Oh, woe,' whined Rex. 'Woe is me. I am a poor hurt doggy and I need someone to open this door and save me.'

'Hello?' the man called again, this time knocking on the door as well.

It took every fibre of his being to overcome his need to bark when the man he labelled 'Sweaty Cologne' knocked. The need to alert when someone came to what he perceived to be his den was wired in at a genetic level. Even when his human wasn't in it, Rex needed to make his presence felt.

He gave another soulful cry, stopping himself from barking by hamming it up a little more.

Another set of footsteps echoed on the floor outside and a new voice joined the first.

'Is that a dog I can hear?' asked the man as he came close. Rex caught a whiff of cinnamon, and cigarettes.

'Yes. I think he might be hurt,' said Sweaty Cologne.

Cinnamon knocked on the door. 'Hello? Anyone in there?'

'Yes, dummy,' sighed Rex, whining loudly. 'There is an injured dog, and he needs you to save him before it is too late. Now open the door, you giant, two-legged, shaved monkey.'

The men started discussing what to do. Rex would have rolled his eyes if he knew what the gesture meant. Instead, he cried some more and flailed pathetically at the base of the door to make it seem like he was trying to get out but was just too weak to do so.

'I'm going to get guest services,' said Sweaty Cologne. 'They can open the door.'

Rex let his head slump. 'Finally.'

'He's fallen silent,' observed Cinnamon. 'Maybe he's okay after all. Perhaps he's just bored.'

Rex whined his loudest. 'Yes, I am bored! Bored of listening to dopey human chatter. Fetch a person with a key and get me out of here so I can solve a crime.'

It hadn't escaped his attention that both the men outside carried the same bay and nutmeg twang from the hotpot. They had visited the hotpot restaurant or had come into close proximity of the dish at the very least. Neither smelled strongly of it, so their brush with the food had to have been passing or several hours ago now.

Convinced by Rex's latest cacophony of heartrending misery from beyond the locked door, Sweaty Cologne ran back to his room to call reception while Cinnamon stayed at the door talking to Rex in soothing tones.

Their conversation, the sound of running in the hallway, and the continued whining brought Constable Dobbs from Mrs Caan's room. In truth, DI Brownlow sent him, mostly so she wouldn't have to tolerate his presence.

He had been outside the hotel, and quite content to be there now the rain had left off, but Sergeant Pike chose to send the inept constable up when he went outside to wait for the grief counsellor to arrive. At such times, it was usual for the officers delivering a notice of death to collect a neighbour or a relative who lived nearby. Someone known to the bereaved was the point, but staying in a hotel room as she was, Mrs Caan said there was no one to call upon.

The counsellor was supposed to have arrived fifteen minutes ago; it was another reason why they'd been hanging around in the hotel's lobby.

Dobbs had a soft spot for all animals, but particularly dogs and hearing one crying now, he refused not to get involved. His instant reaction was to call the hotel reception but upon finding a man talking to the dog through the door, he learned someone was already on route with a key.

Nudging Cinnamon aside, who Constable Dobbs swiftly learned was a member of the TV crew and went by the name Carlton Burrows, he knelt down to talk to the dog.

Rex heard the latest person outside his door and recognised his voice and smell. He wanted to bark for them to hurry up, but accepted he needed to continue his ruse a while longer, impatiently waiting for someone to finally open the door. It was a further three minutes before the assistant manager, Debra Kerr, exited the elevator with a key in her hand.

She was looking stressed and tired. Had anyone looked closer, they might have noticed that she also looked a little merry. Debra's coping mechanism of choice was a hipflask of Irish whisky she kept in her handbag. The manager was away, his holiday booked months in advance, so she was flying the proverbial ship until the duty night manager took over many hours from now, and not enjoying it at all.

A trapped dog was the least of her concerns, but she could see no choice other than to respond and make it look like she was taking the problem seriously.

Constable Dobbs spoke to Rex again.

'Someone's coming now, pooch. Don't you worry. We'll have you out of there in a jiffy.'

Rex heard Debra approaching, identified who it was when he sucked in a noseful of air from under the door, and got to his feet.

The second it opened, Dobbs forced his way in. He was concerned for what he might find and sort of hoped the dog might need treatment so he could busy himself doing that instead of hanging around in Mrs Caan's room with DI Brownlow constantly frowning at him.

Rex went straight between the policeman's legs.

Or, rather, he tried to. Rex judged the gap poorly, so instead of zipping through the gap, he thrust his head between Dobbs' legs, got his shoulders through, but then became wedged.

Sweaty Cologne, otherwise known as Jasper Grainger, was leaning forward to get a look when the giant German Shepherd started running down the hallway with the police officer on his back.

Caught by surprise, Constable Dobbs was facing the wrong way and looking for something he could grab to arrest his motion. Dogs not being built to carry humans, the police officer didn't have to worry for very long because he fell off.

'What the blazes is going on?' enquired Debra, mystified by the dog's dash for freedom. She'd been expecting a half dead animal and an awkward conversation with the owner later. Clearly there was nothing wrong with the dog.

Rex bounded down the corridor, but then something caught in his nose, and he stopped to check it. The scent of the hotpot, not that Rex knew what it was called, was all around him. It was the one smell he was using as a focus for his investigation.

There was a dead human, the cops using the word *murder*, and it all had something to do with the food his human was here for. He'd been running away from the humans outside his room, but running through the air around them, he got a better sense of what they smelled like. The two men – Sweaty Cologne and Cinnamon – had the same undertone and it was hotpot.

Both were staring at Rex in wonder. So too Debra and the police officer who had banged his shin and was trying not to show that he was in pain. It was beyond them to conceive of the dog playing a trick on them.

Rex had no time to explain. DI Brownlow had just opened the door to see what the crashing noise and cries of shocked alarm were. That was all the opportunity Rex needed.

The dog was already running in her direction when she looked down the corridor. Behind her, Mrs Caan was quietly drinking tea; her initial shock and outpouring of emotion had subsided to leave the freshly widowed woman quiet and withdrawn.

That quiet period of reflection ended abruptly when a large animal bounced its way into her room.

'Waaaahh!' squealed Mrs Caan, leaping from her chair and spilling her tea. Horror fuelled her reaction until her brain caught up to let her know it was just a dog.

Detective Inspector Brownlow yelled for assistance, 'Dobbs!' She almost tried to block the dog's entry to the suite as she had last time. However, on his previous attempt to gain entry, the dog had been moving slowly forward from a stationary start. This time he had been running with his head down and her constable was already lying in the hallway looking like he had been bowled over.

Having jumped out of his way, she now followed Rex into the suite.

'What's going on?' Mrs Caan demanded.

DI Brownlow wanted to know the same thing. The dog was sniffing, his nose following a search pattern as he worked his way around the room. It was obvious from Mrs Caan's expression that she expected the detective inspector to eject the dog, but Brownlow was in no hurry to do so.

There was an opportunity that came with the dog's arrival. Would he find something? In the quiet period while Dobbs made tea, she had slipped outside to place a call to the station. The old man was the same one from Dundee.

It was not good news.

Not from where DI Brownlow was standing. She wanted to know why Mr Smith was here and what possible business he could have getting involved in her murder investigation. How was it that he came to be staying at the same hotel? There was altogether too much coincidence for her to swallow.

Nevertheless, she had also discovered the old man's giant brute of a dog was a former police canine. She couldn't call in the forensics team until she had probable cause to do so, and that would only come when she'd had the chance to ask some questions.

To be fair, it was only a little more than an hour since the first call came into the station. She was heading up the case, but it was too early to start whining about not getting the backup she felt she needed.

Her boss expected his officers, especially the senior ones, to manage situations without his needing to hear about what obstacles they had to overcome.

Now that the notice of death was well and truly delivered, and Mrs Caan was settled, she could get someone else in to babysit her and get on with the job of working out what happened.

That was unless (finger's crossed) the dog found something.

Rex wanted to sniff the lady in the chair. He was certain she smelled of hotpot, but he delayed getting to her so he could sort and classify the other smells in the room for elimination purposes.

As he came near, the lady clambered onto the bed.

'Waaah!' she cried again. 'What does he want? Why aren't you doing anything?' Her questions were all aimed at the detective inspector. Brownlow knew she ought to be doing something to get rid of the dog, but it acted as if it knew something.

Mrs Caan crawled across to the other side of the bed, swearing and cursing because the useless detective woman was doing nothing at all to remove the dog.

Unfortunately, turning her back on the dog just encouraged Rex to sniff her derriere.

Rex stopped. He wanted to think for a second. Mrs Caan smelled of hotpot. The distinct scent of the dish had permeated her clothing which, so far as he was concerned, placed her at the scene of the crime. As he understood it, Mrs Caan was the murder victim's mate. He could smell scents on her which were not her own and one of them was distinctly masculine.

The same scent was present in the room he was in, but without Mr Caan to sample, Rex could not correlate what he could smell with the deceased.

Like all dogs, Rex found human relationships very confusing. They mated for life, yet then found a need to mate with other humans while keeping their mating habits secret. Then the life mate would find out and violence tended to ensue. It was all quite bonkers.

However, the presence of hotpot scent on Mrs Caan's clothing didn't make her the killer. It merely made it likely that she was lying about not going to the hotpot place.

'Come along now, dog,' DI Brownlow encouraged Rex to leave. She was being wary, unsure how the dog might react if she grabbed his collar and tried to drag him.

Dobbs had arrived, limping slightly, but putting a brave face on it.

Hearing DI Brownlow address him, Rex looked up at her face. Naturally, his tail wagged and in so doing it wafted the bottom of the bed sheets that draped to the carpet. He was ready to go somewhere else now. The task had been to confirm what his nose believed. Now that he had, there was no reason to stay – he needed to find more evidence before he could figure things out.

The detective lady wasn't looking at him anymore though. Her eyes were locked on a spot behind his tail.

There was something under the bed.

Bluff and Bluster

Albert paused for a moment to collect his thoughts. He was on the opposite side of the street, looking across the road at Parsons' Perfect Hotpots. The amazing smell filled the air still, conjuring images in Albert's head of hotpots steaming as they came fresh from the oven.

How long would it take the smell to fade? Had years of manufacture left an invisible yet flavour-laden coating on all the surfaces up and down the street? Albert pondered these questions and more as he set his jaw and crossed the street.

When he knocked on the glass window of the old, wooden front door, the three heads inside all turned to look his way. They belonged to a young woman, a middle-aged man, and a lady in her seventies. They were the only people in sight and looked to have been arguing until Albert interrupted them.

The man was sitting, the only one of the three not on his feet. He was overweight, but not grossly and Albert took it as a positive mark, the old legend 'never trust a skinny chef' reverberating inside his skull.

If asked to guess, he would say the man was the proprietor, a likelihood made more so when he spoke to the young woman, and she came to the door upon what appeared to be his instruction.

The one thing all three faces held in common was the look of concern etched into them. A man had died in their restaurant and that was not going to do the business any favours.

The door was locked on the inside, the young woman needing almost a minute to wrestle with the top and bottom deadbolts and the lock itself.

The moment she began to open it, Albert started to walk through. He did so without being invited, rudely making the young woman step back to get out of his way. His behaviour was out of character because he was pretending to be someone else. He chose to keep his own name though.

'Albert Smith, Food Standards Governing Body,' he stated. Advancing through the restaurant and passing tables devoid of customers, he maintained his momentum until he got to the seated man and the older woman. 'I believe you are in need of my assistance.' Albert made his face an unreadable mask, his expression set to neutral, but his eyes were hard and demanding – he wanted to make them uncomfortable.

The seated man blinked, questions lining up behind his eyes.

'How are you here so fast?' It wasn't the question Albert had expected, but he fielded it easily enough.

'Chris Caan's demise is all over the internet. You are Danny Parsons?' Albert sought to confirm. Actually, the question was intended to keep Danny on the backfoot – he was less likely to ask questions if he was too busy answering them.

The seated man blinked again. 'How do … Yes, I am. This is my place. This is my mum,' he indicated the lady standing a few feet to his right.'

'Hello,' smiled the older woman. 'I'm Pauline.'

Albert gave her a nod of acknowledgement. Then he hit them with a friendly smile. It shocked them both.

Behind Albert, the young woman finished locking the door again and came to stand beside Danny and Pauline. No one introduced her, but the facial resemblance between the three people told Albert he was looking at three generations of the same family. He would have bet good money

61

the young woman was Danny's daughter. He could find out later. Right now, it was time to learn what had happened.

Since they were still reeling from his sudden change in attitude, Albert pressed them to start talking.

'My purpose here today is not to find you at fault, unless you are …' he let his sentence hang so it invited a response.

'We are most certainly not,' cried Pauline, horrified at the suggestion.

Albert nodded gratefully. 'Then I am here to establish if there is any danger to future customers and get you open again as soon as possible. Why don't you tell me what happened today?' he encouraged.

Danny reacted as if he could scarcely believe his ears.

'You're here to help us? That's not what the Food Standards Governing Body does.'

Albert had an explanation prepared.

'Well, you are both right and wrong on that assertion, Mr Parsons.' He put his clipboard down on a nearby table and started to pace around the room a little. 'The FSGB, as we like to call it, is an independent food safety watchdog set up to protect the public's health and consumer interest in food. Part of that is championing national dishes. Given your status as an award winner, a problem for you is an embarrassment for us. If I can establish the dish is safe to eat and Mr Caan's untimely demise was nothing to do with it … well, let's just say it would be better for all of us. You most especially, I am sure.'

Pauline jumped in before Danny could speak. 'It wasn't the hotpot, Mr Smith, I can assure you. Danny ate some when the police arrived and he's just fine.'

Albert swung his gaze to check Danny's condition. Just fine was not accurate. The proprietor was sweating for a start. It was a cool late autumn day in northern England and the man did not look like he had just been involved in strenuous exercise which might have explained his perspiration. Furthermore, Albert couldn't help but notice that the man was yet to get up and also looked to be in some discomfort.

'Are you?' he enquired. 'Are you just fine? You do not look it.'

'It's just a little stomach distress,' Danny's face coloured, and he held a hand to his ample gut to emphasise his point. 'I had a few too many last night,' he added, providing a reason for his condition. 'It was excitement over the TV show and what it might do for our business.'

'Dad is planning nationwide franchises,' boasted the young woman with pride and excitement.

'This is my daughter, Matilda,' Danny took the hand from his gut to sweep it in the young woman's direction. Moving his limbs turned out to not be the right thing to do. An audible quack erupted from his trousers as his gastric troubles, and the gas they were creating, won their battle to escape.

'Dad!' squealed Matilda, opting to back away a yard. Pauline went with her, both women wafting the air.

Danny looked mortified. 'Sorry,' he mumbled through his crimson face. 'I um …' He pushed off the arms of the chair to get himself upright to the accompaniment of a prolonged gurgle from inside his stomach. 'I'll be right back,' he excused himself, and with a sharp about turn, he started to run for the back of the restaurant.

Visibly trying to hurry, Danny Parsons was walking with stiff legs and clenched cheeks. Before he could get halfway, a noise like thunder emanated from his trousers and he broke into a run.

Albert had not anticipated this.

Questioning if the man would even be able to return, he switched his attention to the two ladies. They had wide eyes and worried looks.

'Perhaps we should carry on without him?' Albert suggested.

Pauline frowned a little, eyeing Albert with more scrutiny than he felt comfortable with.

'You are not like other food safety people,' she pointed out. It was part accusation and part question. 'Are you sure this is all on the level?'

Sensing his ruse was coming undone, Albert scrambled his brain for a suitable response.

'Have you ever met a FSGB agent my age?' he chose to counter with a question and followed it up by answering for her. 'No, probably not. Changes to retirement regulations mean they cannot boot me out. I'll go when I want to, but the years have mellowed me, my dear. Where my younger colleagues will enforce a desist order and prevent firms from trading until they have jumped through a dozen hoops, I prefer to take a softer approach. You should be glad I was in the area today and not Terrible Tony,' he invented a character on the spot.

'Who is Terrible Tony?' asked Matilda with a gasp.

Albert dropped his voice and checked over his shoulder in case Terrible Tony might be lurking in his shadow.

'The worst thing that can happen to a food establishment, that's what. He once shut down a Michelin starred gourmet place an hour before a wedding because a fly flew in through the door. The owner claimed it came in with Terrible Tony, but he forced them to pay to have the premises fumigated in case of an infestation.'

'Cripes,' gasped Matilda.

Locking eyes with Pauline, Albert casually threatened, 'I can call him if you like. It doesn't have to be me here today.'

'No, no!' Pauline raised her hands in defence. 'I was just commenting on how pleasant it is to have you here with us. You're a breath of fresh air, Mr Smith.' She nudged her granddaughter with an elbow. 'Isn't he, Matilda.'

Prompted to speak, Matilda blurted. 'Absolutely. A breath of fresh air.'

Satisfied to have staved off Pauline's suspicions for now, Albert steered them back to the purpose of his visit.

'Now then. Please explain to me exactly what happened in the events leading up to Mr Caan keeling over.'

Pauline asked if she could sit, took a chair at the table nearest to her and with a sigh, she started talking. The TV crew had arrived early that morning, setting up to film the show in both the restaurant and the kitchen. Chris Caan's latest TV show, due to air the next Spring, was all about British food at its finest. His producer, Rachel Grainger, who Pauline referred to as absolutely lovely, could not have been more kind about their hotpot and how it featured so prominently on the list of places to go because Chris Caan was familiar with the area.

Albert stopped her at that point.

'Chris Caan is from Clitheroe?' This was news and Albert could not help but wonder if it might prove to be pertinent.

A toilet flushed somewhere deep inside the back end of the restaurant, but when Danny failed to appear in the next few seconds, Pauline turned her attention back to the man from the Food Standards Governing Body.

'No,' she replied, confusing Albert. 'No, not from here, but he knows Clitheroe,' she clarified. 'Truthfully, I don't know what his connection to the area is. I think he originally comes from Yorkshire.' She frowned in concentration, consulting her memories. 'Actually, I think Danny might have known him. There's a couple of years between them – Chris is older, but I have a vague memory of Danny mentioning him once.'

Albert made a mental note. He would need to quiz Danny about that later. Indeed, it was a great shame the man was not currently present. Had he been so, Albert felt certain Danny's reaction to Pauline's revelation would have told him if there was anything there to pursue.

When asked to continue, Pauline picked up where she'd left off. The TV crew got set up and started filming. They were shooting what they called stock footage for the first hour or so, getting the angles and back drop right for when Chris turned up later.

They filmed Danny making his hotpot and encouraged him to make a big show out of not revealing the secrets of his award-winning recipe.

'What time did Chris Caan arrive?' Albert was getting a lot of detail but nothing he felt was pertinent to the case.

Pauline consulted the inside of her head, but Matilda answered for her.

'It was ten o'clock, gran. Right on time. I remember Rachel remarking about how he is always punctual and such a pleasure to work with. I got the impression a lot of TV personalities can behave like divas and make everyone around them dance to their tune.'

Albert saw a chance to ask a question he wanted an answer to.

'Was Rachel particularly tactile with Mr Caan?' He posed it in a casual manner, hoping it would not seem an odd thing to ask.

'Tactile?' repeated Matilda who didn't know what that word meant.

'He means was she touching him lots,' explained Pauline, her suspicious expression back in place. 'Yes, she was, now that you mention it. What does that have to do with the hotpot though?' She flicked her eyes to his clipboard. 'Shouldn't you be taking some notes? Don't you have to write a report or something. What's with the pen and paper anyway? Don't you all use tablets nowadays?'

'I'm old-school,' Albert replied dismissively. 'You were just getting to the hotpot and what happened to Mr Caan, were you not?' It was a rhetorical question he quickly followed with a prompt. 'Please continue.'

Pauline was chewing her lip in thought, she knew something was amiss or not quite kosher, but wasn't yet ready to challenge the man from the Food Standards Governing Body.

'Mr Caan came ready for filming. A car dropped him off outside, the boy who was here to do makeup,' she made it clear by her tone she did not approve of boys doing makeup, 'checked him over and they started to roll the cameras again less than ten minutes after he arrived.'

'He ate the hotpot?' Albert leaned forward in his chair, finding himself being pulled into the mystery of the man's unexpected death.

Pauline nodded.

'And what happened?' Albert's voice had dropped in volume to almost be a whisper.

Pauline frowned. 'Nothing happened, Mr Smith. Or, at least, nothing unexpected. Chris Caan filmed his piece with Danny. We had a few guests in the restaurant – it was all done before our usual opening hours, but Danny ran a competition to fill the place with winners and drive interest.'

'Dad's such an entrepreneur,' gushed Matilda, glancing at the door Danny had rushed through just as a toilet flushed again.

'Aye,' agreed Pauline. 'He created a lot of interest using some social media site. Anyway, they ate the hotpot …'

Albert jumped in to stop her. 'The same one?' he wanted to confirm.

'No,' Pauline shook her head. 'The one Danny made was for the cameras; the one Chris Caan tasted as they made it, needed longer to cook. The guests got the one Danny made earlier.'

'I see,' said Albert rocking back into his chair as he considered what he was learning. 'Did anyone else eat the same hotpot as Chris Caan?'

'Danny did,' Pauline pointed out indignantly.

'Are you about to tell me he is perfectly fine again?' Albert asked with an edge to his voice.

The door to the restrooms opened and a deflated version of Danny Parsons emerged. His face was pale and his hair messy. Not only that, he now wore different trousers. Albert chose to not enquire as to the fate of the previous ones.

If Pauline had been about to argue that Danny wasn't dead, she chose not to be pedantic when she saw the state of him.

For Albert, who had come here to prove there was nothing wrong with the hotpot, the state of the proprietor was worrying. Maybe the hotpot did kill Chris Caan.

'Are you all right, Dad?' enquired Matilda.

'Just a minor tummy upset,' he replied.

Albert was not convinced but chose not to argue. Not yet.

'Are you well enough to join us?' he enquired.

Danny sagged against the door a little, sucked in a deep breath and propelled himself across the room.

'It's just a minor tummy upset,' he repeated his claim though to Albert's ears it was starting to sound like a mantra.

Watching the hotpot chef as he crossed the restaurant, Albert gave himself a second to think about what he wanted to ask next. There was something already bothering his detective's brain – a piece that was out of place.

As Danny claimed a chair and eased himself down into it, Albert framed a question.

'If the filming took place before you opened. What was Chris Caan doing back here by himself hours later?'

Time for a Stiff One?

Rex turned his head to see what might have caught DI Brownlow's eye, but in so doing he stilled his tail and the bedclothes fell back into place to hide what was there once more.

DI Brownlow knew what she had seen and was going to retrieve it. Unfortunately, that meant getting very close to the giant dog. The same dog who had already given her constable a limp. She didn't fancy an injury of her own.

She wanted to tell Dobbs to move the dog, but he was hanging about in the doorway looking reluctant to come in. Besides, it was no more in his remit to tackle the dog than it was hers.

Mrs Caan was in her bathroom, retreating there and closing the door the moment the dog took his eyes off her.

For DI Brownlow it was the ideal opportunity to have a swift snoop.

Focusing her attention on the dog again, who gave a friendly wag of his tail, she drummed up some courage.

'Move dog,' she commanded, adding a stiff arm jab to the corner of the room to emphasise what she wanted.

'Sure,' said Rex. He got to his feet, moving out of the way with indifference. Sitting on one piece of carpet was much the same as sitting on any other.

The moment he moved, DI Brownlow swooped. Whipping a rubber glove from a pocket, she lifted the bed sheet, checked to see if there was anything else to be found – there wasn't – and retrieved what she had spotted.

'Is that dog still there?' called Mrs Caan from her bathroom.

Brownlow made a guilty face at the dog, then used Rex to her advantage.

'Yes, Mrs Caan. I might need to get animal services in to remove him. I worry he might get aggressive if I try to chase him out.' Her reply – loud so Mrs Caan would hear it in her bathroom – was enough to keep her there.

Sergeant Pike, arriving at that moment with the grief counsellor in tow, came to see what his boss had found.

DI Brownlow turned it around so he could see.

'Viagra?' he questioned, reading the label in such a way that the attractive senior detective could be certain he had never seen the product before and thus needed to read the label in order to know what it was.

DI Brownlow silently lifted a finger on her free hand and pointed to a line on the label.

Sergeant Pike squinted his eyes to read it.

'Who the heck is Samuel Romsey?' he asked.

'That's who the pills were prescribed to with a simple instruction to take as necessary.'

'Good thing the cap was on, otherwise the dog might have eaten them,' Sergeant Pike teed up a joke.

DI Brownlow held a hand up to his face to stop him.

'Not the right place, Sergeant Pike,' she commented disdainfully. In truth, she just didn't want to hear jokes about male appendages.

Rex watched the humans, sniffing the air and trying to work out what they might have found. He didn't recognise the word the man with the beard had said, but even if he had, Viagra and its purpose would have made no sense. Performance issues are not something a dog could grasp.

He questioned for a moment whether there was anything else he might learn by hanging around at the hotel, but decided he was more interested to discover where his human had got to.

The old man was off by himself – never a good thing in Rex's opinion, but more importantly, Rex might be missing out on vital clues his human was uncovering.

'Hey, where's he going now?' asked Sergeant Pike when the dog got up and left the room.

'Where is his owner?' countered Brownlow, cocking an eyebrow at Dobbs as he hung in the doorway.

Suddenly expected to provide an answer, Dobbs hoped it was the right one.

'He wasn't in his room. Just the dog, so I guess Mr Smith went out and left the dog behind.'

Rex paid no attention to the police officers and what they were saying. In the hallway outside Mrs Caan's room, he turned left, paused to sniff the air, and made his way to the door that led to the stairs. Empty spaces such as stairwells carried a unique nothingness smell that was easy to spot if you knew to sniff for it.

The police officer with the beard was calling for him to stop. Rex twitched his head to the side, checking to see what the man wanted. He was following along the corridor, telling Rex to come back.

Rex blinked, made a decision about what he wanted to do, and jumped up to place his front paws on the door to the stairwell. It opened under his bodyweight, pivoting off its hinges until there was a big enough gap for him to squeeze through.

Sergeant Pike couldn't believe his eyes. When he arrived back at Mrs Caan's room and asked what was happening, Dobbs, the utter buffoon, told him the dog had been pretending to be ill so someone would let him out. It was ridiculous. However, if asked to judge what the dog was doing now, he would refuse to admit what he believed – the dog was poking his nose into their murder investigation.

Now the dog was opening doors and taking himself off to wherever it was he had in mind.

'Sergeant Pike?' DI Brownlow's voice echoed out of Mrs Caan's suite. 'Where are you?'

'The dog, ma'am.'

'Leave it.' DI Brownlow wanted to get on with the task of attending to Mrs Caan. 'Send Dobbs,' she shouted as the thought occurred to her.

Dobbs didn't move, unsure what was expected of him.

'Well, don't just stand there, man,' sighed Sergeant Pike. 'You heard the boss. Get after the dog.'

As Dobbs ran for the stairs, he heard his sergeant add, 'You'll catch it in the hotel lobby. It'll never be able to open the front door.'

'What if it does?' Dobbs twisted his body to shout the question back.

Sergeant Pike let a cruel smile play across his lips. 'Then keep chasing it until you catch it, man.'

Busted!

When buying his silly white coat and clipboard Albert questioned his sanity, but now that he had asked the right question, he was glad to have chosen the bonkers approach.

'He wanted the recipe,' Danny revealed. 'That's why he returned by himself after everyone else had packed up and left.'

This was clearly news to Pauline. 'You didn't give it to him, did you?' she begged to know with a horrified tone.

Danny frowned at her ridiculous question. 'I don't like him that much.'

'Dad won't even tell me how to make it,' moaned Matilda. The subject was obviously a sore point.

'When you are ready,' Danny chided.

'I'm twenty-two!' his daughter snapped irritably. 'And I'm not going to leave like mum did.'

Grabbing their attention quickly before they went down a rabbit hole, Albert picked up on what Danny had said about his relationship with Chris Caan.

'Your mother tells me you knew each other as kids?' It was stretching what Pauline had actually said but Albert believed it was more likely to generate an answer loaded with information if posed like that.

Danny gave a half shrug. 'Not really. Certainly not as kids. I met him a couple of times, that's all.'

Pauline frowned, consulting her memory, and looking like hers conflicted with her son's.

'I'm sure I remember you mentioning his name,' she argued, giving her head a little shake. 'Wasn't there a girl?'

A nervous laugh accompanied Danny's next words. 'No. No, nothing like that. You are misremembering it, Mum. Anyway, I can assure you if there had been a girl, it would have nothing to do with Chris Caan dropping dead in my restaurant. I think the autopsy will find he had an underlying heart condition or something.'

'They won't find something wrong with the hotpot?' Albert probed.

'Certainly not,' Danny insisted, acting insulted at the mere suggestion. 'I ate it myself to prove the point. If you are about to question my upset stomach, it is hardly the same thing as dropping dead.'

Albert got to his feet. 'I need to see it.'

'Sorry, the police took it all,' Danny made an apologetic face. 'I think they were just being thorough. They said they needed to check it … analyse it, whatever. Sorry, there's none left.'

Matilda jumped to her feet. 'Yes, there is, Dad. The one you fed Mr Caan this afternoon was taken away, but there were others from the same batch. In all the excitement you forgot to put them in the pantry and left them by the back door where we put the ones to be thrown.'

'Well, I didn't think they were good enough to go to the public,' Danny protested.

Matilda tilted her head in question.

'Dad, they are perfect.'

'Nah, I slipped with the seasoning. There's too much, um.' He stopped talking suddenly and faked a laugh. 'Ha! I almost gave away one of the secret ingredients.'

Matilda looked ready to ask why her father was acting strangely but chose instead to head for the kitchen.

'Either way, Dad. I rescued them and they are in the refrigerator. I forgot to mention it to the police earlier,' she made an 'oops' face. 'They took what we thought was everything, but those ones are still there plus the overflow that wouldn't fit in the pantry, of course.'

Danny's face reddened. 'Oh, err, really?'

Albert spotted the proprietor's reluctance to hand over the hotpot, but kept his mouth shut.

'I'll get them, Dad,' Matilda was already on her way to the kitchen.

Danny bolted after her, moving fast for a bigger fellow, especially one who had until a moment ago been holding his gut and acting convincingly like someone in great discomfort.

Albert went after them, Pauline on his heels.

Just before they got to the kitchen, someone knocked on the front door. Albert threw a glance at the door only to find the sun had fallen in the last half an hour, turning twilight into dusk and then the blackness of a late autumn night. Walking into the kitchen, the nature of the unknown visitors left his mind; he was too enraptured by his investigation to give it any thought.

Pauline, however, peeled off to see who it was.

In the kitchen, arriving just a few seconds after Mr Parsons and his daughter, Albert found them arguing in front of a large refrigerator. The doors were open, and Danny had two small ceramic dishes in his hands.

'Those are the wrong ones, Dad,' Matilda all but stamped her foot. 'The ones you want are these ones.' She lifted a dish from the next shelf down.

'Sweetie,' Danny spoke down to her as if she were being particularly simple. 'I think I know which hotpots are which. These are the ones from the batch I fed Chris Caan this afternoon.' He held up the ones in his hands and turned to look at Albert. 'On any other day, they would be eaten by now. We serve over three hundred every day.'

'Dad, you've got the wrong ones,' Matilda continued to argue. 'You marked the ones you made for Mr Caan with a sprig of rosemary in the corner.'

Danny flared his eyes at his daughter – an unspoken message that she was supposed to understand but clearly did not.

Albert opened his mouth to ask Danny what was in the hotpot – it was clear he was attempting to keep the truth under wraps, when Pauline's voice stopped him.

'There're two gentlemen at the door.' She was glaring at Albert. 'They say they are from the Food Health Governing Body.' Her eyes were cold, hard, and accusing.

Quick as a flash, Albert replied, 'Did I not say I had colleagues coming when they were free? Did they give you their names?'

Folding her arms and refusing to break eye contact, Pauline said, 'Jarvis Dale and Tony Wylie.'

Matilda gasped in horror. 'Oh no! It's Tony the Terrible.'

Doing his best to fake his way through the next sixty seconds, Albert nodded and gritted his teeth.

'Yes, it is. I feared this might happen. Listen, Tony always plays hardball, but he and I are the same rank, and he respects me. Go out there and let him in, all of you,' he gestured to the kitchen door with his head. 'I'll come out once he is inside. He probably doesn't know I am here. It will throw him off balance and then I'll try to get him to see things your way.'

Danny sagged and gasped, 'Thank you, Mr Smith. Thank you so much. This place, what we do, it's everything to us. And there is nothing wrong with the hotpots. Everyone will see that soon enough when the police, or anyone else, analyse them. We don't need the negative publicity. People will think "Where there's smoke" and that could be the end of us.'

'Go,' Albert urged them. 'It will be all right.'

Danny was looking at his hotpots still, worry etched across his face.

Albert shooed him away. 'Nothing will happen while you are gone. I will protect them, but maybe it would be best if we told Tony the police took all the hotpots and pretend these are not here.'

Danny's face looked like that of a man who was holding an insurmountable bill in one hand and being offered a winning lottery ticket to take with the other.

Pauline continued to eye Albert with deep suspicion until her son hooked her elbow and pulled her through the kitchen door.

Albert felt guilty to be sure, but he also believed Danny Parsons was hiding something. There were too many alarm bells ringing in Albert's head for him to consider ignoring them. As quick as he could, he grabbed one of the hotpots Danny had replaced on the shelf he took it from, and another from the shelf below – the ones Matilda insisted were the right ones.

Stealing a handy tea towel to wrap them in, Albert ran as fast as his old legs would carry him, found a back door to the premises, and let himself out. His subterfuge was about to be discovered, but when they looked for him, all they would find would be empty spaces where two stolen hotpots had once sat.

'A life of law enforcement and now petty theft,' Albert tutted as he rounded a corner with a quick check over his shoulder to make sure the Parsons' were all still inside.

As his eyes came back to his front, an expletive burst from his lips and he almost dropped the hotpots.

'What have you got there?' asked Rex, his nose straining forward to sniff the package his human clasped to his chest. 'What is it? What is it? Is it food? It sure smells like food.'

Rex had arrived in the hotel lobby ahead of Constable Dobbs and just as Rachel Grainger was leaving. He followed her out unnoticed by Sue behind the reception desk or Rachel who had other things on her mind.

Once in the street, Rex had to guess which way to go – the scent of his human had faded already, but he figured the hotpot place would be easy enough to find so he tried there first. It was pure luck that his route of approach led his nose to the rear of the building just as Albert was scurrying away.

'How did you get here?' Albert wanted to know.

Rex was trying to sniff the package in his human's arms. The old man had food. The same food from the same place they tried but failed to get into earlier.

'Better yet,' Albert amended his question. 'How did you get out of our room? I locked the door.'

'Never mind all that,' said Rex, attempting to attune his human's attention to more important matters. 'Are we going to eat these now or later?'

Albert had to let go his precarious package with one hand to swat at the dog's nose. Rex was nudging the bottom of the towel in which the hotpots were wrapped, threatening to spill them. To be fair, that was probably his intention, Albert realised.

'We can't eat these,' he wagged a finger in Rex's face. 'One of them might be poisoned.'

'Yeah, yeah. You just want them for yourself, human,' scoffed Rex. 'How about if you stop with the excuses and start with the sharing?' He gave the package another nudge with his nose.

This time, Albert had to juggle the towel and its contents, using both hands to prevent it from spilling.

The sound of voices coming from around the corner ended the discussion.

'He must have come this way,' growled Pauline, disgruntled to have been duped.

'Who was he?' asked a man whose voice clearly wasn't that of Danny Parsons.

'Some random old man pretending to be from your organisation,' she snapped back irritably. 'He even had one of your coats on.' Her voice was getting closer, driving Albert to hurry to the next corner. He could already tell he wasn't going to make it.

Rex was dancing along at his feet, walking sideways and threatening to trip him. Albert questioned if that was the dog's plan.

'A random man in your kitchen, eh?' noted the unidentified man, one of the Food Health Governing Body representatives. 'That's another code violation right there.'

The sound of Pauline's advancing feet halted abruptly.

'What? How could we have known?'

Albert sidled around the corner and out of sight, breathing a sigh of relief as the bickering continued behind him.

A little out of breath from rushing plus the adrenalin of being pursued after committing a crime, Albert slumped against the wall to let his pulse return to normal.

Rex nudged the hotpots again.

'It's going to be hard to focus on sniffing out clues when you are carrying those around. Really, for the sake of our investigation we should get them eaten.'

Albert frowned down at his dog, who wagged his tail in expectation and raised a paw to bat at the package trapped between his arms.

'One day they will invent a translation device that lets humans hear what their pets are saying. I will admit that it would be most useful some days, but I also worry it might scare me to know what is going through your brain.' Albert adjusted his grip so he could ruffle the fur on Rex's neck. 'Seriously though, we need to get these analysed because one of them might be poisoned.'

Rex eyed his human with great scepticism.

Reading his expression correctly, Albert opted for a peace offering.

'How about if we go to a pub, eh? It's getting on for dinner time, I am not about to get the hotpot I came here for,' Albert wondered quite how he might manage to go into Parsons' place now even if it did reopen during his stay, 'and I bet they will have an acceptable version of the dish there. What do you say?'

Rex tilted his head to one side as he tried to decipher all the words his human just said.

Albert didn't wait for a reply. He just started walking, telling Rex about Danny Parsons' odd behaviour, gastric distress, and his suspicions about what might have caused it. When they passed a bin, Albert balled up the white coat and stuffed it in. As a prop it had served its purpose, but he doubted he would find another use for it.

Rex listened in while the old man chattered, loping along beside his human as they ambled back to the main road. There, Albert snuck a look around the corner of a building, saw no one in the street outside the restaurant where he imagined they might still be looking for him, and hurried in the opposite direction.

Mercifully, that was back toward the hotel, and he knew there were pubs along the way.

An Unexpected Ally

With no leash to keep Rex in check, Albert worried about their route along the side of the busy road. It was one of the main arteries through the town – it had to be given the number of cars going by every minute – but Rex plodded obediently by his human's left leg, which placed the old man between him and the traffic.

'Good boy,' Albert cooed for the tenth or twentieth time.

Rex's ears had twitched the first few times the old man spoke, wondering if 'Good boy' was to be followed up with a treat. When no treat came, he stopped listening.

They passed two pubs on the opposite side of the busy road, Albert ignoring them both to avoid the drama of trying to cross with Rex off the leash. Ahead was another one. It was a generic, franchise pub; the kind Albert deliberately avoided at all other times. Today it would have to suffice.

It was quiet inside, the lunch crowd long gone and the evening punters yet to arrive. The pub was not, however, devoid of life.

Albert was only a yard into the building when he spotted Constable Dobbs looking both bored and dejected at a table by himself. The only person in the bar, Dobbs had a half-finished pint on the table to his front and an empty packet of peanuts by his phone, which sat face down and ignored by his right hand. He was out of uniform; finished for the day, it would seem.

Now attired in a pair of dark denim jeans and a back hooded sweatshirt with a black ballcap, he looked right at home in the public house.

The inept constable looked up to see who had come in and reacted as if jabbed with a cattle prod when he saw the old man and the dog.

Albert's lead foot paused as he was about to take his next step. Instantly feeling a little awkward and uncomfortable, his immediate reaction was to leave and go somewhere else. That response lasted all of about a second before he dismissed it.

To start with, leaving because there was someone here who didn't like him would be cowardly. More than that, Albert remembered how many poorly motivated or badly trained officers he met in his time and how it was the senior officer's responsibility to make something of them.

As his lead foot came back to the floor, he changed his direction and went directly across the room to Constable Dobbs' table.

'What do you want?' the young man sneered unpleasantly. 'You and that dog caused me no end of bother today.'

When he had arrived in the hotel's lobby to find the dog gone, he spent the next fifteen minutes searching for it. Accepting defeat and bored with the task anyway, he trudged back up to let DI Brownlow know. He expected yet another dressing down, but all he got was a dismissive wave of her hand. He was no longer required and should return to the station.

His shift was due to finish in half an hour, so he presented no argument, and knocked off early. Now he was in one of his favourite places – he liked it because the other officers never came in here and the beer was really cheap – but now adding insult to injury, the dog he was sent to find had found him.

Refusing to react to the young constable's surly tone, Albert kept his tone affable when he said, 'To help you.' It would be so easy to mirror the young man's poor attitude, and he needed to rise above it. 'May I please join you? Perhaps you would like another beverage?'

Dobbs had been about to tell the old man to sling his hook, but the offer of a free drink was enough to sway his decision.

'I'll have a JD and Coke,' he replied without saying please or thank you. If the old man wanted to spend his money, Dobbs wasn't going to stop him. He could down the free drink, finish his pint, and leave the daft old git behind. He looked up when he realised the old man hadn't moved yet.

'Let's wipe the slate clean and start again.' Albert reached out with his right hand. 'Albert Smith.'

The constable looked at the hand for a moment before deciding he had no choice but to accept it.

'Dobbs,' he replied, giving Albert's hand a weak grip.

'Just Dobbs?' Albert enquired curious. 'No first name.'

'Just Dobbs,' insisted Dobbs, refusing to make eye contact.

Wondering how bad the man's name could be, Albert told Rex to stay, leaving him at Dobbs' table while he went to the bar. He ordered food, got the spirit and mixer for the constable, a bowl and a half pint of Guinness for the dog, and an IPA for himself.

Dobbs mumbled, 'Thank you,' when Albert slid the drink across the table, then picked up his phone to pretend he needed to use it rather than make conversation.

'Why are you so terrible at your job?' Albert asked, posing the question in a polite tone as if it were a conversation starter.

Dobbs spat out the sip of JD and Coke he'd just taken, spluttering dark liquid over his hand and onto the table. When he put the glass down, glaring at Albert, there was a drip hanging from his nose.

Getting in quickly before Dobb's ire could rise, Albert added, 'I ask because it seems that you don't want to do well, like you are choosing to perform badly.'

'You've got some nerve,' growled the young constable. 'What do you know about anything?'

'I'm a retired detective superintendent.' Generally, Albert kept his past secret, especially when talking to serving police officers. He would only reveal the truth if it served the situation. Right now, he needed Dobbs to know not only that he wanted to help, but that he could.

Dobbs pulled a face and sneered.

'Right. So you think you know it all? Just like that cow, Brownlow.'

'What I think I know,' Albert countered rather than rising to the bait, 'is that you can reverse your position, and the DI's opinion with just a few clever moves.'

Dobbs raised an eyebrow.

'Such as?'

Albert took a swig of his beer and poured a little more of the Guinness into Rex's bowl. If he put it all in at once, the dog would drink it in a handful of seconds.

'Well, for starters you could assist the investigation by uncovering something useful. It can be tough at the top, which is where DI Brownlow is going if I am any judge. You can use your eyes and ears to peel back the mystery behind Chris Caan's death. That will gain you recognition and challenge how people perceive you.'

'Everyone thinks I am useless,' Dobbs admitted, glaring at the table, and flicking a peanut crumb across the room with an annoyed finger.

'You can change that,' Albert promised. 'It won't even be difficult to do. Just turn up smart and on time tomorrow and have something to offer that the rest of the team hasn't considered.'

Again, Dobbs frowned and said, 'Such as?'

Albert had been leading the rotund constable towards this point since it occurred to him at the bar. He needed to get the hotpots analysed, and he wanted to find out what the detective inspector might know.

Originally, his desire had been to clear Parsons' Perfect Hotpots of any suspicion so they could reopen. Now, having been there, he wasn't so sure they were entirely innocent. He felt involved now; the familiar tug of a mystery demanding he snoop and sniff until he worked out who was to blame for the TV chef's demise.

He could have badgered one of his children to get him the information he wanted and arrange to get the hotpots dissected. Using Dobbs while simultaneously helping him to overcome his ineptitude felt like a superior solution.

'Well, it just so happens that I interviewed Danny Parsons and his family already. There is something odd about Chris Caan returning to see them this afternoon.'

Dobbs' forehead creased; he didn't know any of this.

Albert spent the next few minutes explaining about the hotpots and Danny Parsons' stomach issues. In his opinion, the very fact that Chris

Caan returned to the restaurant by himself after the filming had finished was suspect enough. The reason Danny gave for Chris Caan returning was even more dubious.

'They knew each other when they were younger,' he revealed.

Dobbs picked up his pint and took a swig. 'Really? Is that important?'

Albert shot him an imploring look, hoping the police officer would begin to piece things together. When he didn't, Albert helped him along.

'A man drops dead in a restaurant, and it turns out that the dead man and the restaurant owner knew each other years ago. Does that not sound suspicious at all? The police suspect he might have been poisoned, so the restaurant owner eats the hotpot to prove there is nothing wrong with it. However, a short while later, he is suffering from gastric issues. Is that not suspicious? Not only that, when I asked to see the hotpot in question, the restaurant owner attempted to give me the wrong ones – at least that is how it seemed on reflection. That is why I have two of them.'

Dobbs' face was screwed up with disbelief. 'You think the owner of Parsons' Perfect Hotpots made a poisonous hotpot to kill Chris Caan? What for? Something that happened when they were kids?' It was clear the constable was struggling to buy a word of it. 'Then what? Danny eats the same poisoned hotpot to prove it isn't poisoned? Surely he is about to die if that is the case.'

'Exactly that,' replied Albert. 'Unless Danny Parsons knew about the poison and was able to take an antidote or something to counteract its effects. It made him ill, but isn't going to have the same effect it had on Chris Caan.'

'What about the wife?' Dobbs questioned. When Albert showed he wasn't following, Dobbs explained, 'I heard the DI and Sergeant Pike talking about Mr Caan's wife. There's some twisted love triangle going on apparently.'

Albert had to nod his head but used the uncertainty to his advantage.

'Exactly, Constable Dobbs. The DI bought Danny Parsons' ruse when he ate the hotpot. She isn't looking at him at all. The love triangle thing could be a complete waste of her time. Imagine how pleased she will be if you are able to present her with a solution to the case because you looked into it in your own time?'

'My own time?' Dobbs repeated the words, trying them on for size because he had never before considered working unpaid overtime of his own volition.

'Yes,' replied Albert with a nod. 'We can start right now, if you like.'

The sound of Rex bonking his head on the underside of the table brought Albert's eyes around to see a man approaching with a plate – dinner for him and Rex.

The man laid the plate down, pointing out a counter across the pub where Albert could find condiments and cutlery.

Rex sniffed the air, his nose at the edge of the table. It did not smell like the hotpot at the restaurant they almost went in.

It didn't look like it either. Albert was trying to feel excited about his dinner, but the plate of food was several degrees south of appetising.

'Franchise food,' he grumbled.

'Don't eat it,' advised Dobbs. 'I never eat here. The food is terrible.'

'But you are in here,' Albert pointed out.

'That's because the beer is dirt cheap.' Dobbs downed the rest of his pint and started to get to his feet. 'Come on. There's a place around the corner that serves a great hotpot. It's my uncle's pub. He'll have one in front of you in under five minutes.'

Marvelling at the change in attitude, Albert gulped down the last quarter of his own drink. Dobbs had gone from unfriendly and uninterested, to collaborative, cooperative, and motivated in the space of a single conversation.

As they left the pub together, his franchise hotpot untouched, Albert felt an upwelling of positivity. He was going to solve the mystery of Chris Caan's death, but in so doing, he was going to help a struggling constable turn his career around.

Yeah, that's not what happened at all.

A little more than an hour later, Rex and Albert were leaving The Queen's Head with their bellies full, and their hunger sated.

Albert could not state whether the hotpot at Parsons' Perfect Hotpots was superior, but the one he had just eaten was as good as any his wife had ever made. It had been a big portion too, which was just as well because Rex insisted on sharing.

It was well after the dog's dinner time, Albert having planned to return to Rex in the hotel hours ago, so the quarter of the dish Rex ate was justified in his opinion.

Dobbs had eaten too, his uncle providing the dishes free of charge after some argument on the subject. To counter his generosity, Albert left a hefty tip.

During their meal, Dobbs listened as Albert talked more about police work and his career, and then about his recent escapades in Stilton, Arbroath, and other places. It turned out Dobbs had heard about them all.

While Albert fell silent to eat his meal, his latest sidekick continued to talk and proved to be an encyclopaedia of knowledge when it came to beer and the other beverages on offer. When the subject cropped up, seemingly by accident, Dobbs rattled on nonstop for over twenty minutes, talking with passion and excitement. Albert wondered if the man might have missed his calling.

It was more than that though. Dobbs acted as if Albert were the only person to have ever taken an interest in him and his attitude continued to improve. So much so, in fact, that outside the pub, he was the one who wanted to get on with things.

93

'Where do we go now then?' He wanted to know, excitement sparkling in his eyes. 'To Parsons' to see if we can catch Danny hiding the evidence? Or back to the hotel where both the widow and the other woman in the love triangle are staying?'

Truthfully, Albert wanted to go back to his room and have an early night. He was still fatigued from the adventure in Dundee and had either been travelling or snooping around since he left the Scottish city this morning.

However, now was not the time to crush Dobbs' enthusiasm, so he sucked it up and picked Parsons' hotpot place. He expected it to be closed anyway. The food health people would have left by now so he could waste a few minutes there and then head for his hotel. He would pick things up with Dobbs in the morning when, hopefully, the constable had been able to catch up on what, if anything, the detective inspector might have learned.

When Rex stopped to sniff something in the street, Albert saw the flaw in his plan.

'I need a lead for Rex,' he announced, puffing out his cheeks as he questioned what he might use.

'Your belt?' suggested Dobbs.

It caused a smile. Albert unzipped his coat and reached inside, pulling the left strap of his braces to show the constable. He expected the obstacle to be enough to put Dobbs off any further adventures, but he was happy to be proven wrong. The man who lacked all motivation earlier provided a solution to Albert's quandary.

'Oh. Um, well, how about mine?' Dobbs fiddled with his waist, pulling his right hand away a moment later with a belt dangling from it like a long, thin snake.

Rex cocked an eyebrow but accepted his fate when the old man gestured for him to come closer. Ten seconds later, man and beast were tethered to one another. It was not a perfect solution, but it would suffice just as long as Albert didn't want to let go in a hurry. The buckle end was looped around Albert's wrist to secure it, and the other end was roughly tied to Rex's collar.

When visiting new towns on this trip, Albert had made a point to explore as much as he could. Walking Rex made that easy in some of the smaller villages they had stopped in but heading back to Parsons' Perfect Hotpots for his third visit, he covered the same roads he'd seen enough times already today for them to become familiar.

His hips were beginning to protest from all the walking. His knees too, and Albert knew that if he didn't stop soon, he would ache all the more the following day. Once he'd indulged Dobbs' desire to be proactive, Albert planned to get a bath and read his book for an hour. It would cap his day nicely.

Approaching the restaurant, the front façade was dark as they expected it to be. Albert didn't want to go any closer, just in case Pauline, or anyone else, were still inside and about to leave.

Dobbs went forward instead, placing his hands either side of his face to block out the light as he looked inside.

'There's no one here,' he claimed, turning away.

Albert gave a tug on Rex's lead to spin him around. 'We'll check around the back.' He was going through the paces, nothing more. The restaurant was all locked up, the owner and staff long gone, and they were not about to break in to snoop around. In five minutes, he would be done and able to get back to his hotel.

Dobbs jogged to catch up, slowing to Albert's pace as they walked to the end of the parade of shops and followed it around to get access to the back.

It was Rex who heard it first.

The sound of two men arguing wasn't loud, but once Albert realised what it was, he also knew where it was coming from.

'That's Danny Parsons' voice,' he blurted, expecting Constable Dobbs to explode into action.

Dobbs stared at the old man. 'Is it? What are they saying?'

There was less light around the back of the buildings where only a couple of security lights and the moon provided any illumination. Thus it was no surprise that Albert couldn't see the men, but he didn't need to. The back of the Parsons' restaurant was thirty yards away and that was where they had to be.

'Get away from me!' shouted Danny Parsons. He was frightened and that made the incident ahead a probable assault or worse.

The dopey constable still hadn't reacted, so Albert slapped him on the arm.

'Go, man!' His insistent, yet hushed command, shocked Dobbs into motion.

'Nobody gets to do that to me and live to talk about it!' barked an unseen voice. It was a deep rumbling bass that suggested the owner was a large man. The accent was local, Albert observed, which probably, but not definitively, made him Caucasian in this part of the world.

The sound that followed was a horrible outrush of air – the noise you get when someone is punched hard in the gut.

It was followed by Danny crying out in pain leaving no question as to who was in trouble.

Rex was quivering, his muscles bunched and ready to go. Had he not been tethered to his human he would already be running. He couldn't tell yet, but it sounded like a perfect opportunity for a game of chase and bite. It was his favourite game, and he was great at it, but he needed to get to the source of the disturbance first; only then would he know how to react.

Driving forward with his paws, Rex dragged Albert along the rutted gravel surface behind the row of small businesses.

Albert was shaking his head. Not at Rex, who was only doing what Albert expected him to do, but at the constable, who was running but not covering a lot of ground. In his day, police officers, especially the younger ones, were expected to be fit. One might allow that the chief constable wouldn't be tearing after criminals and could allow his waist to expand a little, but Dobbs was slow even for a bigger man.

Not only that, he was also holding onto his trousers with one hand and that had to be slowing him even more.

'Police! Stop!' he commanded, reaching the back of Parsons' Perfect Hotpots.

His words caused a shocked expletive and the next thing Albert heard was fast footsteps as someone ran away.

'Hey! I said stop!' yelled Dobbs, running after the shadowy figure as it shot into view and then vanished between two parked cars.

Dobbs yelled again.

Albert wanted to let Rex go, but the stupid belt was all kinds of tight now with Rex yanking on it.

He shouted, 'Ease up, Rex!' pulling the dog back to create some slack.

A shadowy figure emerged on the other side of the parked cars moving at three or four times the speed Dobbs could muster. The silhouette was that of a man, but not a big one as Albert predicted. Rather, the black outline was both short and thin. He ran away from them, pelting down the street with his arms and legs pumping.

Dobbs lumbered out from between the cars, doing his best to give chase even though there was no chance he would ever catch the man.

Albert finally got the buckle end of the belt to slip over his wrist.

Rex felt the tension in the belt go slack and there was nothing to hold him back. When his human shouted for him to go, he was already driving off with his back legs.

Albert sucked in a deep breath as his dog shot into the dark. The shadows on the ground swallowed him instantly, but he doubted he needed to worry about Rex. Danny Parsons on the other hand was worryingly quiet.

Rushing the last ten yards to get to the back of the restaurant, Albert's eye caught sight of Dobbs. The man had taken his hand off his trousers to better create speed, but in so doing, his beltless bottoms had drifted south and were now falling around his knees.

Rex was about to go around the hefty cop when the man fell over, tripped by his own garment.

The dog saw the man falling, his brain supplying the calculation of distance, time, and comparative velocities to reach an unavoidable conclusion – they were about to collide.

Rex was going too fast to alter course in the available time. His only option might have been to jump upward, but Dobbs was falling through the space he would need to fill with his leap.

Albert winced as overweight cop shadow and streaking dog-shaped shadow combined into one with ear-splitting consequences.

Rex yelped in both shock and pain.

Dobbs cursed loudly, hitting the ground and the dog at the same time. With his trousers around his ankles, he scuffed both knees on the loose gravel, banged an elbow and his forehead, but was mostly worried the dog was going to retaliate and bite him.

The man they were chasing heard the commotion behind him just as he reached his car. It was unlocked, but he paused to stare at the moonlit tangle of man and dog, questioning why the person pursuing him had taken his trousers down.

Just what was he doing to the dog?

A groan from somewhere in the shadows to his rear snapped Albert's attention back to the potentially wounded Danny. He could already see Danny's attacker getting into a car; there was nothing anyone could do to stop him getting away now.

The sound of the car's tyres spewing gravel as the driver stamped on the accelerator came while Albert bellowed for Rex and searched for Danny.

He found the stricken restauranteur a moment later. Much like earlier, the man had a hand clamped to his stomach. This time, though, he was using it to stem the blood coming from a stab wound.

There was a lot of blood. Too much, in Albert's opinion. A major artery runs through the gut carrying blood to the legs. If the knife had cut it with anything more than a small nick, Danny was in deep trouble.

'Hold still,' Albert soothed, placing his own hand over the wound. 'Try to be calm. Help is coming.'

Far from getting a bath and an early night with a book, Albert knew he wasn't going anywhere anytime soon.

Dobbs used his mobile phone to call the station, reporting the incident himself. He got an instant response, the sound of distant sirens filling the air less than thirty seconds after he hung up.

Danny was still losing blood, but he was conscious, so Albert hit him with the most obvious question.

'Who was it, Danny? Who did this to you?'

Danny lifted his head slightly and crunched his stomach muscles which forced more blood out of his wound. 'Cactus,' he wheezed as Albert shushed him and tried to get him to stay still. 'Cactus.'

Concerned about the blood spilling from Danny's wound, Albert did his best to soothe the man; he needed to lie still until paramedics arrived. He was losing a dangerous amount of blood, but they would have plasma to give him intravenously through a central line. That would keep him going until they got to hospital.

'Cactus,' Danny mumbled again, his voice nothing but a whisper lost on the wind as he lost his fight with consciousness.

Rex limped over to stand beside his human. His right front paw was bruised, squashed when Dobbs rolled on it.

Albert called for Dobbs. 'I think he just passed out. Try to rouse him. He'll do better if he is awake.'

Dobbs had his belt back on. He'd retrieved it from the dog's collar after making the call for help. The last thing he wanted was guys (or girls) from the station turning up and his trousers to fall down again. He hoped there was no CCTV footage covering the carpark. He would be the laughingstock for years to come.

'Did I hear him say something?' Dobbs asked as he came to one knee next to Danny's head. 'What does cactus mean?'

Albert sucked on his teeth. 'I think he's delirious.'

Dobbs slapped Danny's face. 'Wake up.'

'My God, man!' Albert would have spat out his false teeth if he had any. 'Where did they teach you first aid?'

'What?' Dobbs had no idea what the old man's issue was. 'I'm trying to wake him up. Slapping my face would wake me.'

'I'll have to remember to try it,' growled Albert, shocked at how incompetent the man was at everything. He was beginning to understand how DI Brownlow came to speak so harshly to him earlier.

Before either man could say another word, blue and white strobe lights began to bounce off the buildings. The first squad car had arrived.

An ambulance rolled in right behind them, allowing Albert to breathe a sigh of relief. In seconds he was being carefully shunted to the side so a trained professional could take over. His hands were covered in blood, his clothing stained though he expected it to wash out. Albert's bigger concern was for the victim.

Rex wasn't a fan of the smell of blood. It had a coppery tone that irritated his nostrils and made it harder to discern other scents. While he accepted that he was going to have to suffer it sometimes, he chose to avoid it when possible.

Having backed away to watch his human from a safe distance long before the police showed up with their flashing lights, his nose caught another smell.

A familiar one. One he'd been smelling ever since they arrived in Clitheroe. With his human distracted and his mouth beginning to salivate, Rex set out to find its source.

'Will he survive?' Albert asked when he simply couldn't contain himself any longer.

He got no reply from the paramedics, not to his question at least. The duo, both men with trim dark facial hair were working fast, but they were not dumb enough to commit to an answer.

Instead, the one nearest Albert asked, 'Are you this man's next of kin?'

'No,' he admitted solemnly. 'His name is Danny Parsons. I know that much. The restaurant right there is his place.' A worrying thought crept up his spine and he grabbed for Dobbs' arm.

'Ow, what?' complained the constable.

'Danny's daughter and mother. They were both here earlier. You need to grab the officers who just showed up and have them search the premises.' Dobbs blinked and his mouth opened and closed. 'Show some initiative, man,' Albert begged. 'Lead them. Take charge. You were the first officer on scene, not one of those. Give them the registration number for the car the attacker drove off in, for goodness sake.'

'The car's number? How was I supposed to see that?'

Albert stared at him with a slack jaw. He'd approached Dobbs because he saw a chance to do some good; to help the man, but the task of making a good cop out of him was starting to look like a mammoth undertaking.

'I saw it,' he hissed. 'Write this down.' Albert recited a partial registration number which was all he'd seen, then repeated his instruction to have the premises searched. He could not have made it any simpler or more straight forward, but as Dobbs got to his feet, uncertainty evidently ruling his heart, another car pulled into the loading yard behind the row of businesses and DI Brownlow got out.

'What are you doing here Dobbs?' she asked, her tone leaving no question that she disapproved of his presence.

The man's lips flapped a couple of times.

'Constable Dobbs is here following up a lead, DI Brownlow.' Albert got to his feet as he made his statement. 'I believe he has something of worth to tell you. He was just about to hand over the plate number for the car Mr Parsons' attacker escaped in, but first he wants to get into the restaurant to check for any other victims.'

It was the best Albert could do. If Dobbs couldn't take the baton and run with it now, well ... Albert thought he might just have to throw in the towel.

Dobbs never got a chance to prove himself either way, because DI Brownlow wasn't fooled for a second.

'If Dobbs is doing all that, why am I hearing your voice and not his, Mr Smith?' She dismissed them both with a turn of her head. 'Sergeant Grey, take Sumner and Gough. Go check the restaurant. Watch for evidence of a break in!' she shouted after them. 'Until Mr Parsons regains consciousness, we won't know what motivated this attack.'

Albert bit his lip, stopping himself from pointing out the obvious and logical conclusion that tonight's violent attack had to be linked to the Chris Caan's death.

'Dobbs,' DI Brownlow crooked a finger in his direction. 'Give me that registration number. Then tell me about this mystical lead you think you've found.'

Now on the spot, Dobbs did as requested, reciting the partial number plate and giving the car's make and model and colour.

Albert had to correct him. 'It was an Audi A4,' he said with a sigh. 'Not a BMW 3 series.'

'Are you sure?' Dobbs questioned.

'Was it black?' DI Brownlow asked sarcastically. She had an eyebrow hitched at Dobbs but looked to Albert for confirmation.

He nodded.

'Can I assume the supposed lead Dobbs is here to pursue is your lead and not his?'

Albert acknowledged to himself that she was perceptive and intelligent. She was also tenacious which meant, in his opinion, Brownlow had all the characteristics for the job, and she was going to go far. Despite that, he blew out a frustrated breath and started to argue.

'I don't think you give him enough credit.'

She chuckled derisively at Albert's words.

'Constable Dobbs is here, isn't he? It might be the case that I saw reason to snoop at the scene of Chris Caan's death, but I didn't pursue Danny Parsons' attacker. That was Constable Dobbs.' Albert moved closer, lowering his voice. 'In my day, senior officers pushed their subordinates to grow and learn, we didn't belittle them and rob them of their motivation.'

'I doubt you ever had anyone as incompetent and incapable as Dobbs to work with,' she shot back, holding Albert's gaze, and challenging him to continue arguing. After a second or so, she nodded to herself. 'In your day,' she repeated his choice of phrase. 'I know about you, Mr Smith.' she made a point of accenting the *mister* hard. 'Why don't you tell me what you think you know, why you were back here tonight, and why Mr Parsons, a man I dismissed as a suspect in the case, is now fighting for his life.'

As if on cue, the paramedics lifted Danny into the air on the gurney so the wheels popped out underneath to support it. Then they did their best to not bump him as they rolled him the few yards to the back of their ambulance.

He was still unconscious, and the paramedics remained tight lipped about his chances. Albert did not take these as good signs.

The police got an instant hit on the car registration number. It was registered to a man called Jack Marley – Albert assumed the *cactus* Danny mentioned was a nickname - and it was a black Audi A4 just as Albert said. The address was local, and cops were on their way there already.

Albert chose to sit side on in the back of a squad car, insisting that he needed to rest his legs. He was only sort of playing on his age as a factor because he genuinely was getting a little sore from all the walking and standing around.

Somewhat protected from the cool autumn air, and more comfortable now that he was sitting, Albert explained about the poison in the hotpot.

'There is a connection between Danny Parsons and Chris Caan – something from their youth,' he revealed. The DI didn't have to say anything in response, but Albert could tell by her eyes that she hadn't known.

'I don't know whether that is a factor or not,' he continued. 'I was cut off before I could delve any deeper. However, Danny Parsons was acting suspiciously.'

'Suspicious how, exactly,' Brownlow wanted to know.

Albert sucked on his lips for a second, wondering if he was going to have to reveal his daft disguise and subsequent hotpot theft.

'He ate the hotpot to prove there was nothing wrong with it, right?'

'Yes.'

'He got sick afterwards though. Did you know that?'

Brownlow was beginning to feel resentful of the old man's interference. She was looking at the widow and Chris Caan's producer, Rachel, and Jasper as her suspects. She was yet to prove it or force a confession from either woman, but she believed Chris Caan was having an affair with Rachel. That gave the wife motive, so too Rachel's husband.

Now, Mr Smith was uncovering elements of the case she had not considered, and it made her feel like she was failing in her job. Was this what he had done elsewhere? Did he turn up just as a case surfaced, find a flaw in the investigation, and then exploit it? She found his wealth of knowledge troubling. What was his deal?

'Do you have any evidence that Mr Parsons got sick due to eating the hot pot?' She gave Albert a second to answer, certain he couldn't possibly say yes. 'An upset tummy does not equate to poisoning, Mr Smith. I see no reason to connect one with the other. I am more interested to learn why Mr Parsons was attacked this evening.'

While his human talked in the back of the police car, Rex had sniffed out the source of the heavenly scent. It was the hotpots his human had been carrying around for the last two hours. Albert had abandoned them on the ground when they disturbed Danny's attacker and they were there still.

The tea towel covered them still, but not for long.

Rex remembered that his human didn't want him to eat them, but for the life of him, as drool began to leak from the corners of his mouth, he could not recall why. Resisting food when it presents itself in such a manner is a skill few dogs ever acquire.

Rex was not inclined to even consider doing so.

A few yards away, Albert continued to push the detective inspector.

'Why did Chris Caan come to Danny's restaurant this afternoon? He returned hours after the filming ended and all by himself.'

Brownlow employed an age-old trick to turn Albert's question back on him. 'Why do you think he came?'

'I doubt it was to get Danny to reveal the secret recipe. That was the explanation Danny gave. You need to look at what connects the two men.'

DI Brownlow raised an eyebrow. 'I need to? Mr Smith you have no justifiable reason to be involved in my investigation. Whatever nonsense you are filling Dobbs' head with will prove to be a waste of time. So if this is some strange pet project you have, as you cling to a career that must be just about lost from sight in your rear-view mirror, then I suggest you let it go. My team will apprehend Mr Parsons' attacker, and I will get to the bottom of who killed Chris Caan without your help. Are we clear?'

'Crystal.' Albert knew a natural reaction to the dressing down he was getting would be to become unhelpful where possible. Instead, he asked, 'Do you wish to see the two hotpots I took from the kitchen?'

Brownlow almost told him no but stopped herself because she knew it would be childish. The old man was being more than reasonable, even if he was sticking his nose where it wasn't needed.

It was just at that moment, when he was waiting for her to respond, that Albert noticed he no longer had the hotpots with him. In a flash of memory, he recalled placing them on the ground. It was just when Rex started tugging to get to the man running away in the dark.

His blood went cold. 'Rex!'

Thar She Blows!

The detective inspector offered no resistance when Albert begged for a ride. She was glad for the chance to be rid of him, truth be told, and swiftly assigned a uniformed constable to take Albert to the local emergency vet.

Dobbs went with him, as glad to get away from his boss as she was to see him depart.

In response to Albert's pleas, the driver, a young constable called Fields, hit the lights and put his foot down.

Rex couldn't understand what all the fuss was about. One moment he was licking the second hotpot plate clean, savouring every last grain of flavour, the next everyone was shouting and getting excited.

'It's no good asking to share now,' he'd tutted while backing away from the empty dishes.

His human was worried about something, but it wasn't until the old man said the word 'poison' that Rex remembered the warning he gave earlier.

'It tasted okay,' he pointed out, licking his lips again for good measure. 'They both tasted about the same, in fact.'

Albert couldn't understand the noises and gestures Rex made, but even if he could have, he was too worried to listen to the dog's opinion.

That was why, five minutes later, they were pulling up outside the vet's.

Mercifully, the vet was having a quiet evening – emergency work by definition not based on appointments, it could be as quiet as it could be hectic. This was one of the quiet nights.

Rex was rushed into the surgery, his natural reluctance to go anywhere near a vet overruled by his human who employed Constable Dobbs to help carry Rex.

Plonked unceremoniously on the tiled floor, Rex frowned at Albert.

'What exactly am I doing here?' he wanted to know.

Albert paid him no attention at all, he was too busy explaining himself to the vet.

'I feel fine,' Rex argued. 'If anything, I feel full for once. This daft diet malarky messes with my sleep. A nice meal, that's the ticket to a sound snooze.'

'I don't suppose you have any idea what might have been in the hotpot, do you?' the vet, a man who introduced himself as Mike Farrell, enquired, scratching his head.

Albert pulled a face. 'None at all. Nothing fast acting, I guess.'

A door opened on the far side of the small surgery, a man in his thirties wearing green scrubs poked his head through.

'Do you need any assistance, Mike?' he asked.

The vet turned his head. 'Suspected poisoning,' the two words told the new man all he needed to know. Almost absentmindedly, he said, 'This is my colleague, Simon Varnes. He's the other vet here.'

'I'm not poisoned,' Rex assured them, wagging his tail to demonstrate how good he felt.

Dobbs told them, 'It was the same stuff that killed Chris Caan earlier today.'

The vets both stared at him. 'Chris Caan?' questioned Mike.

'The TV chef?' asked his colleague.

Albert rolled his eyes. The news of Chris Caan's demise had not been officially announced. Okay, it was out there anyway because of the internet, but a police constable ought not to be talking about it. He most especially should not be telling people what might or might not have happened.

Before Dobbs could say any more, Albert said, 'Yes, Chris Caan died earlier today after filming a piece for his new series at Parsons' Perfect Hotpots. There is no reason to believe the two things are related though.'

Mike the vet raised an eyebrow and frowned. 'Then how come you are here with a suspected poisoning by hotpot.'

Albert had to admit the vet had him on that one. Thankfully, before he was pressed for an answer, Rex's stomach gurgled audibly.

'Was that the dog?' asked Dobbs.

Rex twisted the upper half of his body around to look at his back end. His stomach gurgled again.

Mike the vet moved in to check on the dog. His colleague, since he had nothing better to do, went with him.

'Um,' Rex whined quietly. 'Actually … my belly does feel just a little off now that you mention it.'

Mike pulled at Rex's jowls, exposing his gums to check their colour.

Rex was beginning to feel a little more pressure than he wanted to admit, and it was moving toward his tail.

'Um, I might need to go outside,' he whined.

The vets were conferring; the dog wasn't showing any sign of being poisoned. In fact, he appeared to be in great health. Apart from some bloating around his gut, which was to be expected if he'd just scoffed down two whole hotpots, there was nothing to suggest there was anything wrong at all.

They stood up and turned back to face the owner.

Rex got up too. He was getting worried. There was an accident brewing in his belly.

He whined and went to the door. 'Hey, dopey bipeds, if you don't let me out soon, you might regret it.'

Two yards away, the humans were discussing whether the owner wanted them to keep the dog in for the night, just for observation. They could conduct a more thorough examination, but in their opinion, Rex was in no danger.

Albert breathed a sigh of relief.

'I should check his temperature,' Mike the vet commented.

Rex barked. 'Now humans! Really, really right now! We have a code brown situation. There is something going on inside the dog, and it's about to be on the outside!'

Dobbs looked at the dog with both eyebrows touching his hairline.

'What's got into him?'

Recalling the incident in Cumberland, Albert said, 'He's not a fan of the thermometer.'

Dobbs nodded. 'Because it goes ...' he made a gesture.

Albert, less than pleased with the graphic nature of Dobbs' hand animation, simply nodded.

'Yes, because of that.'

Rex was spitting bullets, clenching as hard as he could with all that he had. Even so, he knew he was about to lose.

'This is it humans!' he gasped through teeth clamped tightly shut. 'Don't say I didn't warn you.' Rex rested his head against the wood of the door, something he badly wished he could be on the other side of, and accepted defeat.

'Waaaah!' squealed Dobbs, dancing backward. In a cartoon he would have jumped in the air for Albert to catch like a baby.

Several expletives filled the air, the four men all gaping, eyes agog at the horrifying mess now coating the surgery floor.

Mike the vet murmured, 'I think there might have been some kind of laxative in the hotpot.'

Albert needed to speak but did not want to open his mouth and really didn't want to draw a breath. Nevertheless, but using his coat as a filter, he sucked air into his lungs before blurting, 'Perhaps I should take him outside.'

Rex snapped his head around, narrowed eyes accompanying his indignant glare.

'Oh, sure, take me outside now. That will help.'

Not needing anyone to agree with his proposition, Albert went to the door, stepping around the growing pool of putrid liquid and collecting Rex on the way.

The second the door started to open, Rex stuffed his head into the gap, using his skull as a wedge to force it open. There was more to come, and he wanted to be somewhere else when that happened.

The door, torn from Albert's grip, swung in a wide arc. Its trajectory was going to take it right through the swamp coating the floor like a windscreen wiper sent to hell.

The vets, Dobbs, and Albert all screamed a silent, 'Noooooooo!' but none of them could move fast enough to stop it as the bottom edge did its best to create a wave of terrifying liquid.

The vets bumped against each other in their haste to be somewhere else, both running through the surgery's rear door to get to the back rooms beyond.

'Nurse! Nurse!' Mike called for assistance. 'There is a minor clean up required in surgery two.'

Albert went after Rex. Discretion being the better part of valour, he opted to avoid all questions by collecting Rex and going outside.

His dog was at the glass doors that led to the carpark, panting and huffing while his stomach made noises like a washing machine attempting to contain a volcano.

Once outside in the cool autumn air and gasping because he'd been holding his breath for the last thirty seconds, Albert sucked in a wonderful lungful of crisp, clean air.

Rex was nowhere in sight, but for once Albert's opinion agreed with that of his dog because smell was currently his strongest sense and the one being assaulted. He didn't need to see Rex to know where he was, the odour Rex was producing was what one might call distinct. For that matter, Albert could unfortunately also hear where Rex was. It was not something to celebrate.

Inside the surgery, the two vets were losing an argument with their staff.

Dobbs appeared from the dark, coming from Albert's left, not the direction of the Veterinary building.

'Where have you been?' asked Albert with a frown.

'I scarpered out the back,' Dobbs wheezed, a little out of breath. 'The vets have got a riot on their hands. They expect the nurses to clean the mess up and they are flat refusing. There's a big woman in there who just threatened to shove a wooden handle up their backsides and use their heads to mop the floor.'

'Everything all right?' asked Constable Fields, emerging from the squad car. The stench-laden air hit him in his next breath, reducing the young constable to a coughing, retching mess as he fought to get back into his seat and close the door.

Dobbs skewed his lips to one side and made a questioning expression with his face.

'You think maybe we should scarper?'

Albert choked. 'You're a police officer, Dobbs. You're seriously proposing we just leave rather than go back inside and face the music?'

Dobbs nodded vigorously. 'Yup.'

Albert puffed out his cheeks. 'Good idea. Let's go.' He would call later and pay his bill; he would never try to stiff them on that but going back inside to the toxic environment and the fight raging inside – they could both see wild gesticulations from both sides through the glass front of the building – that did not appeal.

'Rex?' Albert called into the night. 'Rex, are you done?'

Feeling rather deflated, but a lot better than he had, Rex gambolled back into the light of the carpark. Behind him there were patches of grass and a couple of bushes currently ruing the day they bothered to start growing.

'We are getting back into the squad car,' Albert warned. 'Are you quite certain you are done?'

Rex wagged his tail, stopped to consider the question for a few seconds when his stomach gurgled again, but decided there couldn't be anything left in him to come out.

At the car, Albert made sure the dog's back end was as far away from him as possible and settled into his seat with the dog's front paws and head on his lap.

As the driver pulled away, his thoughts turned back to the mystery of Chris Caan's death and the troublesome events surrounding it.

'Laxatives,' he said aloud.

Constable Fields found the old man's eyes with his rear-view mirror. 'What's that?'

'It looks like the hotpot was laced with laxatives. That's what made Danny Parsons so poorly. It wasn't a deadly poison, at least I don't think it was. Rex seems fine now that he has had a thorough cleaning out. But the question that throws up is what did kill Chris Caan?'

'They found a bottle of Viagra pills under his bed,' Fields revealed. 'But they didn't have his name on them. Sergeant Pike said he was most likely taking them to keep up with that producer lady but needed a friend to get hold of them for him so his wife wouldn't know.'

Rachel Grainger. The name echoed in Albert's head. 'Do you know if she admitted to the affair?'

Fields shrugged, clicking his indicator on to turn left at a junction.

Albert fell silent, running ideas through his head and matching them up to what he knew. A TV chef had filmed an episode of his forthcoming show, then returned to the restaurant many hours later all by himself. He was known to the proprietor who was now in hospital …

'Any news on Danny Parsons?' he asked.

Fields shook his head. 'Last I heard he was in hospital and being treated. He isn't dead yet, that much I can say. If he were we would know about it because this would be a murder enquiry and that gets bumped up the priority list.'

'What about the man I chased?' asked Dobbs. 'Did they get him?' Dobbs knew better than to trumpet about the fact that he chased someone. To start with, he got away.

'No one home. They have his picture being circulated and his car will get picked up if he goes near anywhere that has number plate recognition software.'

Albert knew about this development; his youngest son, Randall, waxed lyrically about it one night over a bottle of red wine more than a year ago.

It was relatively old technology, but the infrastructure to support it and the funding to put it in place just wasn't there. It was rolling out slowly, and the police were connected so if Mr Jack Marley were to drive under a camera, they would know about it.

However, catching the man didn't interest Albert. He wanted to work out where Jack Marley fitted into the puzzle.

Refocusing on the pieces, he considered Mrs Caan. Albert would have no reason to suspect her at all were it not for both the Graingers pointing a finger at her. Then there was Jasper Grainger, who, if the rumour was proven true, was losing his wife to the deceased, Chris Caan.

That was motive enough for murder.

Danny Parsons, Jack Marley, Emelia Caan, Jasper Grainger … laxatives in a hotpot, secrets from Chris Caan's youth, connections he didn't yet understand, Viagra under the bed with a different name on it, a missing key …

'The key to their room was missing.'

Both cops twisted their heads inward to look at Albert on the back seat. Even Rex lifted his head to see what his human was talking about.

Dropping the Hook

Constable Fields dropped Albert, Rex, and Dobbs back at the hotel. It was many hours after Albert expected to return. He'd been gone since he locked Rex in their room with a plan to return shortly thereafter. He would have done so too had Rex not come to find him behind the restaurant.

Sue was still behind the reception desk.

'Don't you have a home to go to?' Albert enquired in a conversational tone.

He got a tired smile in reply. 'I was due to finish at six,' Sue stifled a yawn, turning away and covering her mouth until it finally subsided. 'Wooo, sorry. That one got a hold of me. The night manager got drawn into all the drama with the police here this afternoon. Someone is coming to replace me soon.' She thought about that for a second. 'Although, I suppose we do shut the reception in less than an hour anyway.'

'I'm sure they will,' Albert replied so he had something to say.

A moment of awkward silence followed. Albert was wondering how to pose the question he wanted to ask - he'd had it straight in his head until a second ago.

Unsure why the men were hovering in front of her desk, Sue asked, 'Is there something else you need, Mr Smith?'

Albert chose to go for broke. 'The spare key to the suite Mr and Mrs Caan have been staying in was missing earlier, has it been found?'

'Oh, yes. It's the strangest thing. Debra says I must be going doolally in my old age, the cheeky so and so. I swear it wasn't there when I looked, but when she checked, it was on the peg like it had never moved.' A thought occurred to her. 'Why do you ask?'

Albert started to move toward the elevator. 'Oh, just making conversation with a pretty lady.' He shot her a cheeky grin.

Sue sniggered as Albert hoped she would – the comment was intended to distract her. 'Oh, stop it. You'll make me blush.'

Constable Dobbs came with him to the elevator.

'Is that it then? Are we out of leads?'

'Far from it,' murmured Albert. 'All we have is leads. Tomorrow, I'll need to speak with Pauline and Matilda; that's Danny's mum and daughter. I expect they will be at the hospital since the restaurant won't be opening.'

'Why do you want to speak to them?' asked Dobbs, his question one born of genuine confusion.

Albert had to blink a couple of times. 'Because Danny Parsons must be involved somehow,' he explained the patently obvious. 'Danny acted strangely when I wanted to see the hotpots, and he got attacked and stabbed. His mum and daughter work with him. They must know something.'

'Right, yeah, I should have thought of that.' Dobbs fell silent, staring at the carpet for a second. 'Hey, do you fancy a pint before you turn in?' he asked brightly.

A decade or more ago, he might have taken Dobbs up on his offer. Tonight, he was just too tired to even consider it.

'I think I'll just call it a night, if that's all right. It's been a long day for me and Rex. I believe he ought to have a rest and I certainly need one.'

Dobbs nodded. 'Of course, of course. Well, see you in the morning then.'

Albert had one foot inside the elevator car. 'The morning?'

'Yes. I'm off rotation now. I've got three days off and … well, I've been thinking about what you said. About being a bit old to still be a constable and that maybe I should apply myself. I quite enjoyed getting involved this evening so I thought maybe I would come with you tomorrow.' He finished speaking and watched Albert's face, trying to gauge his reaction. 'That's all right, isn't it?'

Albert managed a weary smile. Telling Dobbs that he wasn't needed or welcome, would be like kicking a puppy.

'Sure, Dobbs. Sure. I'll see you in the morning. Eight-thirty sharp.'

Dobbs consulted the inside of his head, his eyes swinging upward into his skull a little to engage his memory.

'Yup. Eighty-thirty.' He brought his eyes back to the front, bashing the side of his head with the flat of his left palm as if to shove the information into place.

Albert stepped backward into the elevator, tugging Rex along with him. Dobbs got a final wave goodnight as the doors closed then Albert allowed himself to slump against the wall.

'Rex, I'm not sure I have ever met a person less well-suited to being a cop.' Bumping off the wall with a flick of his shoulder, Albert cast his eyes down to look at Rex. 'How are you feeling, boy? Are you okay?'

Rex huffed a hard breath. 'It's nice that you are showing concern, but I cannot help feeling that you somehow tricked me into eating those hotpots.'

Albert watched his dog in wonder, attempting to work out what message he might be trying to convey.

'To answer your question, I feel drained,' Rex lamented. He had no desire to accurately articulate his current physical state. Suffice it to say he felt like someone had stuffed a Christmas tree into his mouth, roots first, then dragged it all the way through his body and out the back end to effectively clean out everything in its path.

Albert, listening to the grumbling sounds coming from his dog, ruffled the fur between his ears and gave his shoulder a pat.

'So long as you are not poisoned.' Albert did not want to dwell on how he might feel if he returned from his trip around Britain without Rex at his side. The thought of it was too much.

The elevator pinged, and Albert's phone rang at almost the exact same moment. Fumbling in his jacket while shooing Rex out and trying to hold the door open with an elbow, he finally wrestled it from an inner coat pocket to find it was his daughter calling.

'Good evening, Selina.'

Selina was the middle of his three children and the apple of his eye growing up. Each child was a gift, but Selina - slender, pretty, and bright, had brought sunshine into his day every time he saw her. Her brothers, Gary and Randall, were always covered in dirt and getting into trouble. At least, that was his belief for many years until he finally discovered she was more often the ringleader and her siblings the dopey fools buying into her daring plans.

'Hi, dad,' she answered brightly. 'How are things? Where are you now? Is it Clitheroe?'

'Yes, dear.' He was in the hallway outside the elevator, patting down his pockets to try to find his room key, and struggling to hear what Selina was saying because there were people talking loudly just a few yards away.

Rex sniffed the air. He knew the scent of two of the men; they had been outside his room earlier when he was trying to get out. The smell of hotpot was no longer on their clothes, but that was because they had changed.

Rex couldn't tell that was the reason, though he suspected it to be the case – like all dogs, he paid no attention to the removeable pelts humans wore.

The two men – Jasper Grainger and Carlton Burrows – were with four other men. What Rex was unable to perceive was that five of the men were at Jasper's door trying to convince him to leave with them.

They were all going for a beer and unanimously believed the best thing for their colleague, Jasper, was to get out, have a few drinks, and air his grievances to the world.

'Break ups are rubbish, mate,' Carlton employed a sympathetic voice. 'Hiding in your room is the worst thing you can do. You'll see.'

'We haven't broken up,' argued Jasper. 'It's … she just needs a little time. That's all. Rachel will be back tomorrow. You can bet on it.'

Albert was listening to the men and paying no attention to his daughter.

'Dad!'

'Huh?'

'Dad you haven't spoken in over a minute. I've been asking you questions.'

'Nevertheless,' argued Carlton, the apparent spokesperson for the group outside Jasper's door, 'she's not here now and we,' he gestured to the other fellas to include them, 'all feel you would benefit from getting out.'

'Yeah,' said another man, a younger one with dark ginger hair well past needing a cut. 'There's plenty more fish in the sea.' His sage advice received an angry glare from Jasper and disparaging looks from his friends.

Carlton tried a new approach.

'Look, Jasper, at the very least, we need to toast Chris Caan.' He held up his hands in defence when Jasper's expression immediately shifted gear and headed for the angry lane. 'I know you believe he was involved with Rachel; I don't want to get into whether he was or wasn't. A man died and I think it only right that those of us who knew him raise a glass to his passing.'

It was a strong argument well stated and hard for Jasper to fight without coming off as petty.

'Dad!' growled Selina, snapping Albert back to his own conversation again.

He reached up to press the button on his phone.

'I'll call you back in a minute, love.'

'D ...' Selina's voice was cut off abruptly when he thumbed the red button. Something had occurred to him, and he needed to act now if he were to find out if his question had any value.

Jasper just couldn't be bothered to argue any more. In his mind, Rachel could call at any moment. Or she might just reappear at the hotel looking for him. Okay, she had cheated on him – he was one hundred percent certain of that. He even suspected she planned to leave him, but she hadn't and whether it was right or wrong, weak or not, he still loved her and wanted her back. They could rebuild now that Chris was out of the picture and things would be better than before.

'Just a couple, okay? I'm not staying out until one in the morning with you reprobates just because tonight's gig had to be cancelled.'

That's right, thought Albert. They were due to be filming a live cooking event in the square this evening. With it cancelled, they had an unexpected night off, and were away from their wives and kids to boot. Albert guessed they were heading out to have a few more drinks than they normally might.

He couldn't work out how to insert himself in the conversation going on a few yards away; not without seeming intrusive and rude, but he needn't have worried because the opportunity came to him.

'Hey, there's that dog from earlier,' said Carlton, pointing so everyone would see. 'You should have seen him wipe out the policeman. It was spectacular.

Rex wagged his tail. Only once though. The motion of his tail swinging back and forth teased the muscles underneath it and they were a little sore from his recent explosive experience.

Albert frowned down at his dog.

'What did you get up to while I was out, Rex?'

Rex chose to ignore the question.

Jasper recognised the dog, and Albert; the old man had been with the cops when he found Rachel bawling over her dead lover.

'You shouldn't leave a dog alone like that,' he chastised the old man as he slipped on his coat and started toward him.

Albert's immediate response was to argue that Rex was fine to be left, but proving a point was not his aim.

Instead, he dipped his head, 'Yes, thank you. I was out longer than I anticipated.' Licking his lips, Albert dropped the hook. 'Say, I don't suppose you all heard that Danny Parsons, the proprietor of Parsons' Perfect Hotpots was attacked this evening?'

Albert did not for one second think they could know, nor did he suspect them of any involvement. However, he did wonder at what level any of them might be tied up in Chris Caan's death.

Their eyes showed him how surprised they all were.

Carlton, acting as natural spokesman once again, asked, 'What happened?'

'He was stabbed outside the back of his restaurant just a short while ago. I think the police are on their way back here actually.'

'Whatever for?' asked Jasper.

Albert was partially blocking the hallway with his own body, and Rex effectively cut off the rest of it so the film crew couldn't go anywhere without first asking him to move. They would do that soon enough, but for now he had their attention.

'The key to Chris Caan's room,' Albert supplied. 'It was missing earlier. Then it mysteriously returned. It's locked away in the key thing now, but they said they would be able to get DNA off it even if the person who had it tried to remove their fingerprints.'

Carlton frowned. 'Why would that be of interest. I thought Chris was poisoned by something in the hotpot.'

Albert made a big show of shrugging.

'I believe the police are open to explore options. There is something that does not add up about the poisoning.'

'Because the restaurant guy ate it and didn't die?' questioned Jasper.

Albert shrugged again, an exaggerated move. 'When I spoke to the detective inspector leading the investigation earlier, she made it clear there are more questions than answers at present.'

Jasper twitched his lips to the left and right, thinking something he chose not to voice.

Albert watched him intently – the man was one who had a definite motive for murdering Chris Caan. However, Jasper was either able to play it cool, or he was innocent because his face gave nothing away.

Carlton clapped his hands and rubbed them together, a conspiratorial grin splitting his face.

'I rather think we ought to get moving, chaps. I'm feeling rather parched myself.'

Albert hooked a hand through Rex's collar, manoeuvring him to the side so the men could pass him. They were gone a few seconds later and the hallway was silent once more.

Albert scratched his chin and tried again to fit the pieces together. Jasper, Emelia, Danny Parsons, and Jack Marley. There was no question in his mind that Jack Marley had stabbed Danny Parsons though the why of it continued to elude him. Which of the others might be involved, whether it was all of them or none, he ... Albert paused, his brain taking a left turn.

... then there was the name on the bottle of Viagra. Samuel Romsey was yet another player on the field somehow. Was he a complete red herring?

Letting go a long sigh, Albert patted down his pockets once more, found his key, and once in his room with the door locked, he took out his phone and called his daughter back.

He needed to apologise to her. But he also needed to ask her a favour.

While he waited for the call to connect, he looked down at Rex.

'You know, dog, I think this might be a long night.'

A Daughter's Dilemma

Albert's prophecy proved to be self-fulfilling because it was by his design that his usual bedtime got pushed back so far.

Secure inside his room, he listened to his phone ringing and then the voicemail thing telling him to leave a message? Was his daughter ignoring his call because he cut her off earlier? Or was she now busy doing something else?

He had no way of finding the answer, so he made a point of checking on Rex, doing what the vet had to check the colour of his gums and prod the dog's abdomen to see if he was tender or sore.

Rex took it all in. Provided no one came near him with a thermometer, he didn't care too much if they wanted to check his teeth and ears and such.

That it was most probably laxatives in the hotpot was a relief, but it also raised questions to which he worried he might struggle to find answers. The only way the laxatives got in there was if someone chose to introduce them. Albert wasn't buying that it could be an accident. In essence then, Chris Caan had been poisoned, but the intent was not to kill, but to make him ill.

Why?

Albert wanted to quiz Pauline and Matilda; they had to know something. They were bound to be at the hospital with Danny so he could find them too if he tried. All these things ran through his head as he sat on the edge of his bed with Rex's head on his lap.

He stroked the dog's fur and enjoyed the comfort of his company. He wanted to be mad with the daft dog for eating the hotpot and giving him such a scare, but Rex did as any dog would do when presented with something edible. How could he blame him for that?

There was something more immediate to tackle than tracking down Pauline and Matilda. He might get to them in the morning, but worried how they might react to his presence given how he duped them today. Also, if Danny's injuries were worse than Albert hoped, would he die during the night?

He doubted he could justify begging them to answer his questions if the worst happened.

Believing he had a little time before he needed to get into position, Albert stripped out of his clothing and washed himself at the sink. Truthfully, he wanted a bath. He'd been thinking about it all day. A nice soak in a hot tub was always high on his list of personal pampering activities. He had even been known to use a little bubble bath every once in a while.

There really wasn't time for it though, so he made do with what he could achieve.

Rex stayed on the carpet as far away from the bathroom as he could get while still being in the suite. Given how the day had gone so far, Rex half expected there to suddenly be a reason for his human to try to bathe him.

Due to that concern, his eyes stayed open, watching the door suspiciously until his human emerged once more. The bath taps were not running, the old man showed no sign that he might attempt to coax Rex toward the room of wet doom, and Rex allowed himself to relax.

He needed some sleep. Just like Albert, Rex was trying to process what he had witnessed today. A human had died; he got that. It happened at the hotpot place and people believed it was murder. After that, so far as Rex was concerned, it all got a little sketchy.

The hotpots were laced with something that turned his insides into a lake of brown lava. He felt way below par because of it and wondered how long it might be before he wanted to eat again. Then the man at the hotpot place got stabbed. Rex couldn't figure that out at all. His attention was still on the widow of the first victim.

She lied about going to the hotpot place, Rex was sure of that. He just didn't know why.

Dressed again, Albert took a comb to his meagre ration of hair. There wasn't a lot of it remaining, and what there was had lost the dark brown colour he'd once sported, yet there seemed no need to leave it messy.

Task complete, he checked his watch, remembered his need to apologise to his daughter, and retired to one of a pair of chairs arranged next to a low coffee table on one side of the room. The places he stayed were never this plush. Even the hotel he and Petunia spent their wedding night in hadn't been this swanky. Despite that, Albert wasn't sure how they justified calling it a suite.

It wasn't as if it had extra rooms. It was just big. Nevertheless, the chair he sat in was comfortable, and that allowed him to relax which, in turn, demonstrated just how tense he felt.

'Dad,' Selina was distinctly monosyllabic in answering the call.

Pulling an oops face at himself, Albert set out to repair the damage.

'Sorry, love. I was suddenly right in the middle of something.'

'Dad you are always right in the middle of something. We all heard about Dundee you know.'

Albert closed his eyes. He had been very deliberate in avoiding the press that night. They were massed at the police cordon interviewing the owners of over a hundred dogs who had bolted from their homes to join Rex in raiding the warehouse where Albert was being held captive.

Despite that, his name must have appeared on a police report somewhere. Stupid computers. They were to blame for this. His children – each of them senior detectives – would have alerts set up so they would find out the moment any officer in any police department in any county wrote their father's name.

'Dundee wasn't my fault,' he started to explain. However, it felt as if he was making excuses like a young boy in trouble with his mother. He stopped himself. 'Things just happened. I was mostly an innocent bystander.'

Selina said, 'Uh-huh.' She wasn't buying it. 'What is it that you are innocently standing by now?'

Albert burst out laughing. 'Absolutely nothing, dear. This time I am deliberately up to my neck in it.' Before she could question him, he explained about his pilgrimage to Lancashire in search of the best hotpot they had to offer.

'Is it better than mum's?' Selina interrupted him to enquire.

Albert chuckled at the question. 'I have no idea. And that's the point. They were bringing out a body when I got to the place. Did you hear about Chris Caan?'

'The TV chef? Yes.'

'Well, there you go. They think someone poisoned him. I'm hoping to get a look or maybe just some feedback on the toxicology report later.'

'They are going to share that with you?' Selina didn't bother to hide the incredulity in her voice. 'Are you bribing them?'

'I made a friend, Selina. That's all.' Whether Dobbs could get the information or not remained to be seen. He hadn't thought to ask him earlier, but the results wouldn't be back from the lab until tomorrow at the earliest.

Selina rubbed at her forehead. 'Okay, so you are mixed up in a murder investigation.' She put two and two together. 'Oh, Dad, are you really investigating this so you can get the hotpot place open again?'

Miffed that his daughter could read him so well, he mumbled, 'I was. Originally. The chap that owns the place got stabbed an hour ago though, so I don't think that is on the cards anymore.'

His brain was running triple time while he talked.

Selina heard him fall silent and interpreted it.

'You're about to ask me to get hold of a copy of the casefile, aren't you, Dad?'

In truth, the thought was yet to cross Albert's mind, but with the seed now planted …

'Could you, love?' he asked, sugar dripping from his words. 'That would be ever so helpful. There is something happening here, but I cannot for the life of me figure out what it is. Seeing what the police know might help enormously.'

Patiently, Selina said, 'Dad, you know you could just move on and come back in a week's time. By then I bet the hotpot place would be open again. Where are you planning to go next?'

'Blackpool,' he admitted, grumpily.

Selina pulled a face Albert couldn't see. 'Hardly the time of year for it.' She had an image of walking along the promenade with the beach to one side and the amusements, shops, restaurants, bars, and arcades to the other. In her head, the sun was shining down and the smell of the sea wafting inshore competed with the scents of candyfloss, bags of salty chips, and hotdogs. At this time of the year, a person was going to be walking under grey skies and praying they didn't get soaked.

'I am too close to not include it. I went there as a child,' he reminded his daughter.

She smiled to herself. 'I remember seeing the pictures.' Then, tutting because she knew she was going to do exactly the thing she believed she ought to not do, she said, 'I'll see what I can find, Dad.'

They talked for a few minutes more, Albert catching up on what his grandkids were doing and Selina enquiring about Rex. Albert chose to omit the laxative incident from his report.

When the call was over, he stayed in the chair for a few minutes. Albert was tired, Rex appeared to have gone to sleep, and it would have been very easy to climb into bed and call it quits. Unfortunately, such a thing was not in his nature. He did however choose to postpone his next venture.

His excitement had dwindled, and that was allowing him to view things with a calmer set of eyes. There was no need to rush to his next task. In retrospect, he could have run a bath and relaxed in it with little risk of missing that which he hoped to catch.

With a deep sigh, he decided that he was clean now; running a bath after washing himself at the sink was just an indulgence. He settled for reading his book, whiling away more than an hour before he decided it was time.

Stretching and yawning, he put the book down, fetched Rex's lead, and went to the door.

Hearing the familiar jangle of his leash, Rex raised his head. He'd been deeply asleep and happily so.

'We're going out again?' he enquired, not getting up because his human never went out at this time of day. Not unless … 'There's something going on?' he guessed, clambering to his feet.

Albert held the door, then hooked Rex's collar as the dog tried to leave the room.

'This is a stealth mission,' he explained, coming down to one knee so his head was almost at the same height as Rex's. 'For this I need you to remain silent.'

'Sure,' said Rex. 'I can do that.'

'Which means,' Albert continued. 'No snoring in your sleep.'

'Oh.'

'No chasing cats and squirrels in your sleep.'

'Oh.'

'And above all no farting like a dump truck starting up in cold weather.'

Rex frowned. He wanted to claim that he did no such thing, but he was prone to wake himself up and had on occasion then elected to sleep in a different room because the one he was in contained a frankly unexplainable green cloud of funk.

Albert gripped the doorframe and used it for balance as he levered himself back to upright.

'Shall we?' he politely enquired.

Rex took that as his cue, cautiously sniffing the air, as was his habit, before setting off for the elevator.

Following behind, Albert knew he might be committing to lose a few hours sleep in order to test a theory, but he was too curious to let it slide.

Had he known how his night was going to pan out, he would have gone to bed and put a pillow over his head.

Guilty

It was close to one in the morning when the black-clad figure peered around the edge of the door leading out from the stairwell. It was a time when he felt sure everyone in the hotel would be asleep and he could realistically go about his task without being caught.

There was no security camera – there couldn't be, or they would have caught him either taking the key two days ago or putting it back yesterday afternoon. Since they hadn't, it stood to reason no one knew.

The old man's words chimed in his head again - his DNA was on the stupid key. Why hadn't he thought of that?

Checking around in every direction, despite believing he was utterly alone in the hotel's reception area, he sidled out from behind the door and closed it gently and carefully behind him. In a few minutes, he would be back in his bed and safe from the minimal chance the police might knock on his door.

He didn't need to be answering uncomfortable questions or finding himself implicated or suspected of having a hand in Chris Caan's death. His life was already enough of a mess without any additional drama.

The door to the reception was locked. It hadn't been on the previous occasions but that had been during the day when the reception was manned. To both get the key and return it, he'd taken swift advantage of the desk being temporarily unmanned. The second time had been when the police were here. He'd gotten away with it then, and he would again now.

That's what he told himself as he nimbly vaulted onto the reception desk. There, he paused because he thought he heard something and listened intently for several seconds. Squinting into the darkness, he dismissed it as his imagination and dropped down to the tile on the other side.

Like the door to reception, the box on the wall where all the keys hung on their little hooks was locked.

That presented something of a problem, but it was one he'd anticipated and had arrived prepared for. All the film crew guys carried a few tools with them; they came in handy all the time.

A large, flat-tipped screwdriver would do the trick. The damage would be discovered in the morning, but they wouldn't know who had taken the missing key and he was wearing gloves this time so there would be no fingerprints or DNA left behind.

The door to the cabinet popped open with minimal effort. Then, using his torch, he found the key he wanted, removed it from its hook with his glove-covered hands, and slipped it into his pocket.

Pushing the little door closed once more, he wondered if maybe he should take all the keys. That might make it look less suspicious – it wouldn't be just the key to the dead man's room that was targeted.

He didn't get to finish making his decision on the matter for the lights flicked on before his heart could beat again. Bathed in light like a robber in a searchlight, Jasper Grainger felt his pulse spike and a hard ball of guilt formed in his gut that threatened to make him vomit.

Across the lobby, just inside the door of the hotel's small bar, the old man sat on a chair. He was facing the reception desk and had his right arm stretched up to a set of light switches.

The old man's dog was sitting upright next to his chair.

'Smile for the camera,' quipped Albert, holding his phone out. He'd been shooting video for the last couple of minutes. Nothing much would show up on the footage before the lights came on, but he doubted that would matter. He had film of a man wearing rubber gloves and holding a large screwdriver next to a cabinet of keys with a busted door. Good luck to Jasper's defence lawyer.

Jasper had frozen the moment the lights came on, his heart thumping hard in his chest but it lasted only a couple of seconds. The old man speaking broke the spell.

With a burst of energy, he made to leap the reception desk again.

Albert growled, 'Rex, sic 'im.'

The giant German Shepherd dog exploded from his position by the old man's side. One second, he was placid, the next, he looked ready to cause grievous bodily harm.

Jasper had his hands and one foot on the reception desk, his body rising from the floor as he thrust upward. It was all he could do to reverse trajectory before his limbs or face came within reach of the dog's teeth.

Rex barked madly. This was great! A game of chase and bite where the human being chased had nowhere to go! Brilliant! If his tail had wagged any harder, it might have snapped off.

Albert bellowed, 'Rex stay!'

Rex had been about to jump the reception desk to get to his quarry. The desk was way above his head, but far from insurmountable. The human had vanished from sight in a tangle of arms and legs, the man tumbling backward and out of control to evade Rex's snapping teeth.

Now his human wanted him to stop? Rex spun around to check.

'He's right there!' he barked. 'I just want to bite him a little bit. Just to make sure he can't run away again.'

Albert could see how excited his dog was. 'I should stay there if I were you, Mr Grainger. I'm calling the police. If you attempt to escape, Rex is very likely to bite you.'

'I'm going to sue you!' raged Jasper from behind the reception desk. 'Your dog almost did bite me already. I injured myself trying to get away from him. That dog is dangerous!'

'You're damned skippy I am!' barked Rex in agreement.

Jasper had been about to raise his head to lock eyes with the old man, however the fresh fit of barking dissuaded him. 'I'll have it put down!'

Albert merely laughed at the idea. 'You'll go to jail, Mr Grainger. That's what you will do.' The phone stopped ringing in his ear as the call connected. 'Yes. Police, please.'

Less than a minute later, the dispatcher was speaking to the officers in a patrolling squad car less than a quarter of a mile away.

Two minutes after that, they were running up the steps to the hotel's front door.

Simultaneous with their arrival, the hotel's duty night manager, asleep in a small room set aside for exactly that purpose, staggered out.

'What's going on?' questioned Wayne Baptiste around a yawn. His trousers were on with a Megadeath t-shirt above them and a towelling robe over his shoulders to finish his very early morning ensemble.

The police officers hammering on the locked front door drew his attention. With eyes flaring, he scanned around the lobby, taking it all in, though he was having trouble deciphering what he could see.

'What's going on?' he repeated, unable to come up with a different question.

The hammering came again, the police officer nearest the door raising an eyebrow as he shouted, 'Open the door, sir.'

'I think perhaps you ought to do as he requests,' suggested Albert.

'I didn't do anything to Chris Caan,' protested Jasper, still keeping out of sight behind the reception desk.

His unexpected voice made Wayne the sleep-deprived duty manager jump.

'What the heck? What's going on?' he managed for a third time.

The police officer banged on the glass of the door again.

Albert ignored everyone except Jasper. He was out of his chair, glad to no longer need to stay quiet and still. He'd been in it for almost an hour while he waited for someone to show.

His money had been on Jasper, but it was based on nothing more than a gut feeling born of experience. If someone were to come for the key, they would do so in the small hours, setting an alarm perhaps to sneak down while everyone else slept.

His little lie about the DNA was a long shot – a shot to nothing if you like, yet it had paid off.

Crossing the lobby, Albert leaned on the front edge of the reception desk and attempted to peer over. All he could see of Jasper was his feet sticking out. The man was effectively underneath the desk.

'You can discuss what you did or did not do to Chris Caan with the police, Mr Grainger.'

'I didn't do anything to him.' Hearing the nearness of the old man's voice, Jasper ducked his head out from under the desk and twisted around to look.

'Then you ought not to be breaking into the hotel reception to steal keys.' Albert made his point while holding Jasper's gaze. In all honesty, Albert wasn't sure what the man might have done, but he did believe Jasper had motivation. Whether Rachel was guilty of being involved in a sexual relationship with Chris Caan or not, Jasper believed she was, and that could easily drive a man to kill.

Behind Albert, Wayne had the front door open finally, a blast of cold night air sweeping in with the cops as they gladly came inside.

Albert turned to face them.

'You're the gentleman who made the call?' the lead officer asked. Both men were constables, yet the one taking the lead was a decade older than his younger, female colleague. They looked alert and ready, two attributes Albert approved of.

'Albert Smith,' Albert introduced himself. 'This is Rex Harrison,' he used the lead to secure his dog.

The duty manager left the front door unlocked assuming the police would want to exit again shortly and came around them to join in the conversation.

'That dog attacked me,' complained Jasper.

Albert didn't look his way when he said, 'Open your hand.' Jasper said nothing. 'Show them the key you just stole.'

Wayne the duty manager shook his head and frowned. 'What's going on?'

Above his head, his human talked to the police officers. Rex paid them no mind. He was sniffing the air. The gust that blew in from outside carried something on it that was familiar. It wasn't coming from any of the humans in the lobby, it was … something else.

He closed his eyes to shut out his peripheral senses and better focus on the one he trusted most. He'd encountered it earlier today. Recently, in fact. It was a man's scent but contained an earthy note. There was blood too, he realised. Not fresh like from a wound, but not old either. A recent wound then, the blood dry but only just.

The humans were paying no attention to the dog. They were engaged in a fast argument about Albert's involvement and the potential danger the dog represented.

The lead cop, Constable Gunderson, glanced down at the 'dangerous' dog. It was sniffing the air and utterly disinterested in the man claiming it tried to bite him.

Jasper denied having the key, having stuffed it into his pocket when he first saw the police. When assured he would be searched and it would be better for his defence if he came clean first, he relented. However, he continued to deny any involvement in Chris Caan's death.

'I took the key because I wanted to catch Rachel with Chris,' he explained. 'It's been going on for months, but she continues to deny it. I just wanted to catch her so we could get it out in the open. Not being able to prove she was lying was driving me nuts.'

The junior constable standing to Gunderson's right made notes as Jasper spoke.

Gunderson had Wayne unlock the reception door so they could retrieve the guilty man without the need for anyone else to clamber over the desk. Jasper was cuffed and checked for weapons and that was about it.

Albert rubbed at his nose when the officers led Jasper Grainger away. He would be questioned, and his story checked, but Albert wasn't sure what to think. Jasper's sole motivation seemed to be rekindling his marriage. He believed his wife was cheating but rather than appear vengeful, he just came across as sad. Jasper wanted his wife to end the relationship and come back to him.

'Is there anything else, Mr Smith?' asked Wayne around another yawn as the police filed outside pushing Jasper ahead of them.

Albert had been only vaguely aware the man was even there. He shook his head.

'No. Thank you for your help. I think I'll retire to bed now.'

A tug on his lead caused Rex to snap his eyes open. He was still working on the familiar scent he'd found. It was unfortunate that he wasn't able to pinpoint it sooner – he might have been able to stop the cops from leaving and that would have been useful.

Riding up to the top floor in the elevator, Albert's face split in two as the caffeine he'd taken earlier began to wear off. It was hours after his usual bedtime, and he would need to make up for it soon or pay the price. A lie in would help but he'd arranged to meet Constable Dobbs at half past eight so there was no chance of that.

'I don't know about you, Rex,' Albert had to stifle another yawn. 'But I am beat. I need some sleep.'

Rex wasn't paying any attention. The scent that came in on the breeze from outside was long gone again, but he could not shift the belief that he needed to be concerned about it. The fact that he couldn't pinpoint it told him he had never come close to its source.

It was the smell of a man he'd passed or …

The elevator pinged and the doors swished open.

The scent hit Rex's nostrils again and his eyes slammed open. His paws moved on autopilot, driving off the hardwearing carpet floor of the elevator car as he surged forward and into the hallway.

Albert was just taking a step when Rex leapt. His right arm, not prepared for the sudden movement got a cruel yank that hurt his shoulder.

'Rex!' he complained loudly, but not so loud that he might wake people slumbering in their rooms. He didn't say anything else though for there was a figure framed in the hallway ahead and it had a knife.

Rex barked. The sound was deafening in the silent hotel, and it was enough to make both Albert and the man with the knife jump.

Albert hadn't seen the man's face before, but he didn't need to in order to know who it was.

'Jack Marley,' he murmured.

Being named caused a series of questions to fire in Jack's head, but now was not the time to start asking them. He could see the dog was coiled like a spring; its legs were twitching in its desire to attack.

Jack, thrust off with his left foot, twisting around to start running in the opposite direction.

Albert realised instantly where the small man was heading – the stairs were right there.

Rex could not contain himself. This was the man who stabbed Danny Parsons. It was Danny's blood he could smell on Jack's clothing. He didn't need to know the names or understand all the moving parts; all he needed was for his human to either let go of his lead or unclip it from his collar.

His tummy felt awful still, and he was empty of food which meant he was low on energy. Nevertheless, this was chase and bite; his favourite game, and he was a match for any human no matter how poorly he felt.

Albert saw Jack Marley slam into the stairwell door. His shoulder barge sent the door careening back until it hit the wall with a loud crack. Lost from sight a second after the chase started, Albert was trying to get Rex free.

He didn't particularly want his dog to chase after a man with a knife, but Jack could only be here to do harm and Albert already knew, without checking, whose door he had had been standing outside.

Old fingers fumbled with the catch on Rex's collar. It didn't help that the dog was constantly twitching and trying to lunge forward. Albert could have just dropped the lead, but he worried the loop end might catch on something while Rex was running full speed. That such a sharp stop might snap his neck played heavily on Albert's mind.

As the catch came free, there was no need for Albert to yell, 'Sic 'im!' because Rex was already going.

The stairwell door had jammed open, Jack's violent abuse sufficient to break the top hinge. Rex shot through it but the advantage he had on the flat was significantly less so on the stairs. He couldn't go down them as fast as he could run on level ground, and he had to keep turning as the stairs wound round and around going down.

Jack was two floors down and nearing the bottom. He was fast on his feet and jumping to the next landing from halfway down each flight. The dog was not going to catch him.

He could be worried that the old man knew who he was – Jack was able to put two and two together to work out it was the same dog that tried to chase him earlier at the restaurant. However, that he was known to the old man came as little concern; he was already wanted by the police, he had watched from across the street when they showed up at his house earlier.

He didn't mean to stab Danny Parsons; that was an accident. But it was one he couldn't undo. His sole intention was to finish the necessary work he started, and he would have already done so had the old man and his dog not showed up when they did.

Going down the stairs was making Rex puff and pant. He wasn't gaining on the human, which was bad enough, but it was the discomfort in his belly that troubled him the most. Did he need to eat? Or should he never eat again? Whichever it was, he felt terrible.

Despite that, he pushed on. Down and down, step after step as fast as he could.

Upstairs, Albert was calling the police again, but he was doing it against a backdrop of people waking up and coming into the hallway to see what was happening, plus he felt the need to hammer on Emelia Caan's door.

It was her room Jack Marley had been standing outside. Was he on his way in or out? Albert needed to know the answer to that question. There was no blood on the carpet by his feet, and no sign that the door had been forced.

That didn't mean much in Albert's book.

All too many times, he had read about or been witness to attacks that took place on a doorstep. In his mind, he could picture Mrs Caan coming to see who was outside, only for Jack to thrust his weapon at her. She could be on the other side of the door and bleeding out right now for all he knew.

'What the heck is going on?' demanded Carlton Burrows. He had on a pair of jogging bottoms and nothing else, his rotund belly hanging over the top of his trousers for the world to see. He had to blink against the sudden bright light in the corridor and did not look pleased.

'Mrs Caan?' Albert called for the fifth or sixth time. 'Mrs Caan?' He continued to hammer insistently on her door, ignoring Carlton who felt it necessary to repeat his question much like Wayne the duty manager had only with more force and less confusion.

'Here, I'm talking to you!' he snarled, reaching to grab Albert's arm.

'Yes. Your voice travels,' Albert snapped a flippant reply. 'Make yourself useful, man, and break down this door.' The emergency services dispatcher had just connected him to the police, so Albert turned away from the irate, half-naked man to speak to them instead.

Carlton looked at Mrs Caan's door. 'Huh?'

Four floors below them, Jack Marley made it to the bottom of the stairs and kicked the door open. Bursting into the lobby, he failed to break that door, though he did leave a boot mark the cleaner would need three weeks of polishing to fully remove.

The dog was still coming but he had a few seconds. Long enough to make sure it would follow him no further.

Snatching a chair, he flipped it onto its side and stamped down hard on the nearest leg. It snapped off, hanging limply by the last couple of splinters.

A moment later, Jack jammed it under the bottom edge of the door and kicked it in hard with the toe of his boot. A cry of triumphant rage accompanied an expletive-filled taunt as he slapped the door and sprinted for the exit.

Rex neither understood nor cared about whatever Jack had just said. He reached the bottom of the stairs out of breath and feeling queasy yet determined to keep going. The door, however, stopped him dead.

Unnoticed by Jack as he ran out the hotel's front door, Wayne Baptiste, the duty manager, stood in the reception area dunking a tea bag in a mug of water. He was still dressed in crumpled trousers, t-shirt, and towelling robe and wore the same vacant expression Albert and the cops had endured.

He heard the footsteps charging down the stairs, saw the door slam open and watched with a bemused expression as the short man broke a chair and made good his escape.

Talking to himself, he crossed to the door mumbling, 'What is going on?'

Rex heard someone on the other side of the door and managed a bark. There wasn't much behind it, but he was doing his best.

When the door swung open, the man in the towelling robe letting him out, Rex sucked in a deep lungful of air and set off again.

Where is Emelia Caan?

There was still no answer from Mrs Caan and her door was still firmly shut. Albert was having to shout to make himself heard due to the number of people now in the hotel's top hallway. It was almost all members of the TV film crew arguing about what they should be doing and questioning who the old man was.

Albert put his hand over the phone again.

'Just break the door down, will you?' he shouted at the four men gathered outside it.

Two more couples were in the hallway. They were a few yards beyond the scene outside Mrs Caan's suite and nothing to do with what was going on there. In each case, one partner had demanded the other, 'Go and see what all the racket is.'

Subsequently, they got out of bed themselves when they refused to believe the report coming back.

Albert took his hand away from the phone again.

'Yes. That's what I am telling you. Jack Marley, the man wanted in connection with the stabbing earlier this evening, was outside Mrs Caan's door. Yes. Yes, the same Mrs Caan whose husband was poisoned earlier today. He was armed with a large knife and ran when challenged.' There was a pause as he listened, then he said, 'Just send everyone.'

'Emelia?' Carlton Burrows called through her door.

Albert rubbed his forehead with his right hand.

'Look, she isn't answering the door. So either she isn't there or she is dead or dying.' A man down the hallway gasped. 'You need to kick the door in and find out. I'll pay for the damage.'

Carlton looked at his colleagues, several of them exchanged glances, before he shrugged and said, 'On three?'

The door rattled in its frame, but the lock gave up on their third attempt.

Albert had to watch from across the hallway so the men had room, but the moment the lock gave, he darted forward.

The lights came on ahead of him, one of the TV crew hitting the switch as they surged courageously inside.

The bloody scene Albert feared he would find was not there. The suite looked lived in; shoes on the floor, a robe discarded on the edge of the bed. However, Mrs Caan was not there, and Jack Marley never made it beyond her door.

As Albert made his way around the room, Carlton Burrows spoke.

'What's he looking for?' Not getting an answer from any of his friends, he raised his voice. 'Hey, old man. What are you looking for?'

'A handbag, a phone, any indication that Mrs Caan did not leave of her own accord.' Albert had not the faintest clue what was going on. Mr Caan's widow was not in her suite, but what did that mean and where on earth was she? Had she absconded because she was involved in her husband's death? Had something happened to her? The second question begged a third which was all to do with why Jack Marley was involved. Was he alone? Were there other parties? Just what were the Caan's mixed up in?

'I'm getting Jasper,' grumbled Carlton as he stomped back toward the hallway.

'He's in police custody,' Albert announced absent-mindedly while continuing to poke around the suite.

His revelation produced a series of questions, expletives, and confused looks.

Responding to them, Albert said, 'He was arrested after breaking into the reception downstairs. He was trying to steal the key to this suite.'

Carlton couldn't believe what he was hearing. 'Why?'

Albert fixed Carlton with a questioning look, studying the man's face when he asked, 'Was Rachel having an affair with Chris Caan?'

'That's what Jasper believed.' That Carlton's answer avoided giving a direct yes or no was not lost on Albert.

'What do you believe?' he probed.

Carlton didn't really want to answer; it felt like a betrayal, but with all that was going on, he also didn't want to be trying to hide the truth.

'Probably,' he admitted, sounding sad.

The sound of sirens in the street outside ended the conversation and the men in Mrs Caan's suite ran to the windows to see outside.

Outside, Rex was pushing himself to do vastly more than he felt able to. Jack Marley's scent was easy to follow; it was a still night and there was no one else around to mask it or mix it.

Rex was not going at full speed though. His stomach was cramping, the discomfort from it making running close to impossible.

Seventy yards ahead of him, Jack Marley was also out of breath. His car was around the corner from the hotel, but leaving the building in a hurry through the front door, having snuck in through a fire escape originally, he managed to turn the wrong way.

He needed to double back, but the dog was after him, cutting off the route he wanted to take. To get back to it now, he would need to circle a block and hope he could stay ahead of the dog. Or should he abandon the car and steal a new one?

The cops would be looking for it by now, he told himself. All he needed to do was stay ahead of them for a few more hours. Just long enough to find Emelia, that was all he asked for.

Rex heard the police sirens a few seconds before the people in the hotel. He was outside for a start, but he was also closer to them. He couldn't know it, but the nearest squad car when the call came in was the same one that had just left.

Gunderson and his partner were heading back to the station with Jasper Grainger secured on their back seat. They would have ignored the shout if they hadn't seen the small man dispatch was describing. He ran across the road fifty yards ahead of them.

A second later, Gunderson spotted Rex loping along the pavement to his left.

'He's chasing him,' he commented.

'Huh?'

Gunderson ignored his partner and punched the button for the rooflights. The small man was still in the street ahead. How he reacted to the lights and sirens would tell them all they needed to know.

When he spun around to stare at them, and then took off like Carl Lewis, there was no need for Gunderson to give an instruction.

Rex caught up to them a minute later. Flopping to the pavement for a rest, he gave Jack Marley – cuffed and sitting against a wall - an obligatory growl.

'No one outruns me.' It was a half-hearted comment. Rex felt like he had been kicked repeatedly in the gut. He said the words but there was no emotion behind them. Worse yet, he knew he still needed to walk all the way back. He figured he could rest a while first.

Cops had arrived at the hotel. There were four this time and more inbound. DI Brownlow had been woken at home and would be joining them when she could get there, but for Wayne, the duty manager, it was already easily the busiest night he'd ever had.

'Top floor,' he told the officers as they came into the lobby. His tea was half gone, and as the elevator doors closed, he went in search of biscuits to dunk in it. He doubted he was going to get back to bed any time soon.

By the time the officers arrived on the top floor, Albert was in his own suite fetching his gloves, scarf, and hat. Rex was outside somewhere and that gave him cause for worry. The dog had wandered off before.

156

Checking pockets before setting off, Albert recalled losing Rex in Arbroath and York to name just two destinations on their tour of the UK.

'That's him.'

Albert swung his head around as he pulled his door shut to find Carlton in the hallway still. He had four uniformed officers around him and his right arm raised to point an accusing finger. It was pointing in Albert's direction.

It was to be expected. He was the one who placed the call – his second in quick succession.

With his left hand, he tried the door handle of his room to make sure it had locked, then set off to intercept the police.

'Good morning,' he hallooed them brightly. 'Is DI Brownlow here yet?' Acting and talking as if he were in charge of the situation and better informed than they could possibly expect him to be, put them all on the back foot as was his intention. 'I'm just going to fetch my dog. Please let me know when she arrives.'

The cops were massed outside the elevator doors. That was where Albert wanted to go and whether intentionally or not, they were blocking his path.

One, a sergeant with what looked like long blond hair pinned up under her hat, held up a hand to impede his progress. 'Just a moment, sir. I have some questions for you.'

'They can wait until I have my dog,' Albert replied without slowing his pace. He was going to walk right through her outstretched arm if he needed to. 'He's the reason you have one man in custody and another suspect on the run.'

As luck would have it, the elevator pinged before the sergeant could reply, the door swishing open to reveal Gunderson with Rex.

'Rex!' Albert cheered his dog's name upon seeing him unharmed and returned.

'Gunderson?' questioned the sergeant.

'He was chasing the suspect,' Gunderson explained, letting go the dog's collar so he could return to Albert. Focusing his attention on the old man, he added, 'He seems a little winded. He's very lethargic?' It was posed as a question, Gunderson hoping the dog's owner would know what was wrong.

Albert crouched, lowering himself slowly so he could get down to one knee and hug Rex around his shoulders.

'He ate a large portion of laxatives by mistake earlier today. It was in the same hotpot that …' Albert's voice trailed off, a random thought bumping into another one somewhere in the distant reaches of his brain.

'Same hotpot …' the sergeant prompted.

Albert placed the thought in a holding pattern to consider later. There was something about the laxatives that was troubling him. Abruptly realising his face was hanging open and probably making the cops think he was having a stroke, he shut it and forced a smile to appear.

With a nod toward Gunderson, he said, 'Thank you for returning Rex. I don't know what I would do without him.'

Rex licked his human's face.

'Can we get to bed now? I think I need a few hours of sleep to recover.'

Albert, escaping further face washing, pushed himself back to upright. 'You say you caught Jack Marley?'

Gunderson nodded. 'He was running down Queen's Road. He walked right in front of the squad car.'

'Where is he now?' asked the sergeant.

'Penny has him and another chap in the back of the squad car.'

Gunderson's reply prompted her to hand out orders. She didn't want two suspects from what might, or might not, be the same case exchanging notes and ideas in the back on one car. She sent two officers with Gunderson to transfer Jack Marley. All four were to return to the station. Orders given, she turned her attention back to Albert.

'I am going to need to record a statement, sir.'

Albert nodded his understanding. This was not his first rodeo.

It was almost three in the morning when Albert last saw his clock. He had been in bed for most of an hour, staring at the ceiling or the inside of his own eyelids as he fought with the thoughts swirling inside his head.

Sergeant Rossiter – she introduced herself before Albert felt a need to ask her name – was good enough to allow Albert to return to his suite. With the remaining officer standing like a sentry by the door, she and Albert sat on comfortable chairs either side of a small coffee table until DI Brownlow arrived.

It turned out, however, that the detective inspector did not wish to interview Albert herself.

'Take his statement,' she instructed. She was standing in the hallway just outside Albert's room where Sergeant Rossiter had been summoned to join her. Albert got ignored by the senior officer, though he wasn't sure if it was because she didn't want to discuss the case with him – he got the impression she thought of him as an interfering old busybody – or because she genuinely felt her time was better spent interviewing the suspects.

Either way, she arrived, told Sergeant Rossiter what to do, whispered something that she didn't want anyone else to hear, and left again without giving Albert the time of day.

Rex didn't even notice she was there. He was asleep, his body doing its best to reset after the thorough emptying it endured.

Once back in Albert's suite, Sergeant Rossiter listened to his account of events, going back all the way to his arrival just twelvish hours ago.

'Where were you before Clitheroe?' she wanted to know.

He admitted to coming from Dundee and held his breath to see if she would make the connection between the events there the previous day – two days ago now, Albert's brain corrected him – and the man she was talking to.

Mercifully, if she knew about the drugs bust and warehouse raid involving an old man, an older woman, and a pack of domestic dogs, she failed to join the dots.

There was nothing in his account that could raise any suspicion. He started by revealing his past employment and that, in many ways, explained this evening's events. He saw things others might not see, and thought in ways that led him to raise questions others might never consider. Rex was a former police dog – he was on his bed in the corner fast asleep and snoring – which meant chasing down miscreants and pinning Jasper Grainger in place were second nature.

Satisfied, but warning Albert that he might be called upon to answer further questions yet, she got up to leave.

Before she could escape, he pinned her with a few questions of his own. The first was about Danny Parsons. Sergeant Rossiter did not know the stab victim's current condition, which was good enough for Albert, because she would have if he had already died.

It had only been a few hours so he could conceivably still be in surgery. Or he could be out and recovering but still touch and go. Either way, Albert had not been expecting Sergeant Rossiter to tell him Danny was on the mend.

His second question was about the findings of the toxicology report for Chris Caan. This time he got a stern denial.

'Mr Smith the details of that report will not be made public knowledge and I do not see what possible interest you could have in them.'

Albert knew why he wanted to see the report. There was an idea circling in his head all to do with a case from many years ago. He half remembered it – the victim's name escaped him, but he would not know if he was onto something until he got to see the report. Would Selina come through? Or would he be able to work things out regardless?

Only time would tell.

His third question was one that had been bugging him for hours.

'Who is Samuel Romsey?

'Samuel Romsey?' she echoed. She wasn't acting; she'd never heard the name before. Albert swore inside his head because he should have thought to ask Selina to investigate the name when he spoke to her earlier. Far too late now, it would have to wait until daylight returned.

Sergeant Rossiter was clearly itching to get going, but he had one final question.

'Where is Mrs Caan? Has she been located?'

Sergeant Rossiter's right eyebrow twitched, and she nodded to herself. 'Mr Smith, I have been instructed to stick to the task of extracting from you what you know. I am not here to reciprocate with delicate information pertaining to an official police investigation.'

Albert had not expected the official approach. 'I am merely asking as to the health and whereabouts of a woman I know to have been targeted this evening. I see no reason to keep me in the dark.'

'Nevertheless, that is my instruction.'

She wasn't going to say anything else on the matter, so Albert bade her a goodnight, closing the door after the two cops left. It was time to get some sleep.

It just took a while for him to find it.

Waking to find there was sunshine coming through his window – it was so late when he went to bed that he forgot to close the curtains – Albert blinked a few times and tried to work out why his brain was reporting an alarm. He was missing something or had forgotten something and ...

'Dobbs!' Albert sat up in bed, scrambling for his watch to check the time. It was already a quarter to nine. Tired from his day and then late to bed, he'd slept in for the first time in years. Tutting and grumbling to himself because he was never late to arrive anywhere without a desperately good reason, Albert threw on his clothes.

The shower beckoned as had the bath the previous evening. A quick tickle with a wet cloth was all he allowed himself. With teeth brushed and hair straightened, he roused Rex, threw some kibble under his nose, and went out the door.

Rex needed a walk before Albert tried to eat, but he hoped to find Dobbs waiting patiently in reception so he could first apologise. Then perhaps he could entice him to come for a stroll so he could fill him in on all he missed the previous evening.

It hadn't gone unnoticed by either Albert or Rex that he ate his kibble as usual. Hunger was the first sensation Rex felt when his eyes opened. He was keeping quiet about it because he wasn't yet certain how his stomach was going to react to the reintroduction of food.

Albert hadn't mentioned it because his mind was on other things. Why had Chris Caan gone to Parsons' Perfect Hotpots yesterday afternoon by himself? Where was Emelia Caan? Why was Jack Marley outside her room with a knife?

Jasper Grainger was arrested and taken into custody but what part had he played in Chris Caan's death? Was he just a husband trying to save his marriage? Albert couldn't tell, but would guess there was nothing to connect Jack Marley to Jasper Grainger. That being true, then the only thing they had in common was the Caan's. But what about them? The mere fact that Jack Marley was trying to get into Emelia's room hours after her husband died had to mean there was more to this than just Chris Caan. Whatever it was involved them both.

Exiting the elevator with his eyes peeled for Constable Dobbs, Albert frowned when the man was nowhere in sight. He checked in the restaurant, peering through the door as he searched to see if Dobbs might have chosen to wait in there with a cup of tea.

He wasn't there either.

Dismissing it because Rex wanted to go outside, Albert left the hotel, turned left, and made his way to a park he'd spotted upon their arrival the previous day.

Crossing the road, his phone rang. He expected to find it was Dobbs' name displayed on his screen but was more pleased to discover it was his daughter calling.

'Good morning, Selina,' he trumpeted. 'Do you have something for me?'

Rex was pulling at his lead, the scent of squirrels and rabbits in his nose now that they were in a green area. A flash of something to his left, a rabbit tail zipping back under a gorse bush and out of sight was enough to make him forget all thoughts of the investigation.

Albert unclipped him and found a handy bench to sit on. Rex would need a few minutes after all.

'Right, Dad,' replied Selina. At the other end of the line, she was sitting at her breakfast table with a cup of tea and an A4 notepad of scribbled notes. She had abused her position to have one of her own sergeants look into the case while she slept. She had not expected to find much but that proved to not be the case.

'What is it?' Albert coaxed his daughter to start revealing what she knew.

'Well, for a start Chris Caan has a stalker. Did you know that?'

'No.'

'His cars have been damaged on several occasions in the past year and there are reports of his hotel rooms being broken into. The case file is quite extensive.'

'Any suspects?' Albert held his breath while he waited to hear.

'Interestingly enough, yes, Dad. A man called Jack Marley is named in the report. There is nothing concrete to implicate him though. Reading the report, I get the impression Chris Caan named him. It doesn't say why so I did a little digging this morning and found a newspaper report from where you are.' Albert had questions lining up on his tongue but held them in check so his daughter could continue. 'Over in Burnley, just a few miles from Clitheroe he – Chris Caan that is – is credited with ruining Jack Marley's business.'

'What was the business?' Albert had to know.

'He ran a restaurant. I need to dig a little further, but I think Chris Caan went to catering college with Jack Marley. Anyway, Chris Caan wrote a scathing report on Jack's restaurant, the Food Health Governing Body swooped, and his business folded the same month. That was a year ago.'

Albert murmured, 'Jack wanted revenge.'

'Very possibly so. You might be interested to learn that Danny Parsons survived his wound. That is the man you told me about last night, isn't it?'

'Yes.'

'Okay, yeah well, he is listed as critical, but one thing I can tell you is that he is alive. Also, Jack has not confessed to stabbing him.'

'I hardly think he needs to,' Albert snorted. 'They'll get a conviction anyway.'

'That is as may be, Dad, but you know these things are easier with a confession.'

'What has Marley said?'

Selina had been waiting to get to this bit. The transcripts of DI Brownlow's interview with Jack Marley did not take a lot of reading. He refused to speak. In fact, the one thing he did say was when the detective inspector asked him whether he killed Chris Caan. 'He thumped the table in anger and complained that he never got the chance.'

'He never got the chance,' Albert repeated Selina's words. 'He didn't say anything else?'

'Not in over three hours of interview.'

Albert marvelled at the news. He'd had some tricky customers in his time; people who would clam up and refuse to speak. They all caved in the end, every last one of them. In his entire career, he could not recall a suspect going three hours and uttering only one sentence.

'I never got the chance,' Albert said it again. It was like an anti-confession. Albert was certain Jack Marley stabbed Danny Parsons; the why behind would be nice to know, but basically stating he intended to kill Chris Caan but didn't get to ... to Albert's mind, it meant he wasn't the killer.

However, it could also be a very clever line to make them look elsewhere. He would go to jail for stabbing Danny Parsons but the sentence for that would look like a slap on the wrist by comparison to premeditated murder. Was Jack Marley that clever? Albert hadn't met the man – seeing him twice did not count, but his gut told him Chris Caan's killer was still at large.

'Anything on Jasper Grainger?' he asked.

Walking back to the hotel with Rex plodding contentedly at his side, Albert wasn't sure what to think. He was zero for two so far as arrests went. Not that they were his arrests, but he knew what he meant.

Jack Marley wasn't going to get out of custody any time soon. He was guilty of assault with a deadly weapon, grievous bodily harm, and more besides if they could tie the stalking to him. However, Albert had already dismissed him as a suspect in Chris Caan's murder. If anything, poisoning, while dramatic and ironic for a TV chef, seemed also to be out of character and too impersonal for a man with a large knife.

Jasper Grainger likewise had nothing to do with Chris Caan's demise. He was still being held, but no charge had been raised and they would have to release him soon if that failed to change. Albert wasn't ready to scrub him from the list of suspects completely, but he had moved him to the bottom of the list.

He remembered at the last second to ask Selina about Samuel Romsey. The name was an enigma. If he had someone other than Dobbs working with him, Albert might have been able to tap into the local police, but his impression was that DI Brownlow had discovered who Albert was and had then chosen to keep him as frozen out as she could manage.

It was a senseless attitude so far as he could see. A good cop uses every advantage on offer, every resource.

Selina promised to look into it and get back to him if she got a hit.

As he neared the hotel, his head still filled with conflicting ideas about the case, he heard his name being called.

Rex heard it too, swinging his head around to look back along his flank to the man hurrying their way.

'Albert!' called Dobbs, out of breath and struggling to get any words out. 'Albert, wait up.'

Albert stopped walking. He was hungry now and wanted his breakfast. The inept Constable Dobbs was trying his patience. Dobbs was a friendly sort but giving him what felt like a third or fourth chance last night, the man then turned up an hour late for their rendezvous this morning.

Albert didn't say anything, choosing instead to let the man catch up. He wanted to hear if Dobbs had a list of poor excuses for his shoddy timekeeping.

Dobbs slowed to a walk, sucked in a couple of recovery breaths and grinned. 'Woooh, I need to get in shape,' he joked self-deprecatingly. 'Morning, Albert.' Stopping right next to Rex, he bent a little at the waist to greet the dog too. Only then did he notice Albert's expression.

'Wait, did we agree half past eight or half past nine?' Dobbs questioned, his face showing genuine mystery. When Albert failed to respond, he concluded, 'It was half past eight, wasn't it?'

Albert pursed his lips. 'Yes, Dobbs, it was. Are you often late for work?'

Dobbs made a glum face. 'Yeah, all the time.'

Albert choked; the man was so blasé about it. 'Does it not occur to you to leave for work a little earlier? Set an alarm? Perhaps prepare things the night before so you can roll out of bed and go?'

Dobbs frowned, thinking on Albert's words. After a few seconds, he said, 'No.' In the next heartbeat, as if like an Etch-A-Sketch the slate had been wiped clean, Dobbs was smiling and onto a different subject. 'Hey,

169

did you hear they caught and arrested two men last night? One was the fella I chased around the back of Parsons' hotpot place.'

Albert hardly thought what Dobbs did could be called giving chase, but he let it slide.

'I did hear that, yes.'

'So, it's done then. They caught Chris Caan's killer already and it was all down to us. Do you think DI Brownlow will give me any credit?' Dobbs wore an expression that accepted how unlikely he thought it was.

Albert shook his head to clear it. 'Hold on. They did what? What makes you think Chris Caan's killer has been caught. Did Jack Marley confess?'

Dobbs' lips formed a confused O shape.

'Um, he stabbed Danny Parsons,' Dobbs started to explain as if talking to someone particularly stupid. 'That was at the place where Chris Caan was poisoned. Then he turned up at the hotel where Chris Caan's wife was staying and from what I heard he had a big knife with him. Also, DI Brownlow discovered that Jack Marley had been stalking the Caan's and had motivation for wanting revenge because Chris ruined his business. Case closed, so to speak.'

Albert frowned and asked a question. 'Is it you who thinks the case is closed, or everyone?'

Dobbs did not understand the question.

'Um, everyone?' he posed it as a question because he really didn't know what the old man was asking.

'Specifically, please, Dobbs. Has DI Brownlow stopped her investigation?'

Dobbs was starting to find the old man's intensity a little scary.

'I think she believes she has the killer in custody but is still asking questions. To gather the evidence for a conviction, won't she need … I don't know, maybe proof of how Jack got the poison into Chris Caan?'

'Yes, she will,' murmured Albert. His mind was racing again. Jack wasn't going to confess because he didn't do it. More and more, Albert felt convinced Danny poisoned Chris Caan. The intent had not been to kill though, only to incapacitate.

Twisting around abruptly to face the other way, Albert set off at a brisk pace. 'Come on,' he called over his shoulder.

Dobbs, momentarily left behind, ran to catch up.

'Where are we going?'

'We have important things to do. Quite a list, in fact. DI Brownlow has the wrong man, and we need to prove it.'

'That's right,' agreed Rex. 'The wife did it. I've been telling you all along. She was at the hotpot place, and she lied about it. You should ask her why.'

'Wait, what? What wrong man?' asked Dobbs, ignoring the noises the dog was making.

Albert wagged a finger. 'No jumping ahead. We'll get to that. We need to start with the first task on the list.'

Eyes wide, Dobbs begged to know. 'What's the first task?'

'The most important one,' Albert replied mysteriously while waggling his eyebrows. He was already enjoying his day. The local cops had the wrong man; he was certain of it, and if Dobbs was even half right, they were not going to look where they needed to in order to discover they were wrong. He could tell them, but they probably wouldn't listen, and if they did, what would be the fun in that?

The most important task, much to Dobbs' surprise, was breakfast.

Albert maintained that hunger is a distraction they could do without. He had a long list of places to go, information to uncover, and people to find and then quiz. It was going to be a long day, so what better way to start it than with a full English?

Getting Dobbs to join him did not take a lot of effort.

Two heaping plates of sausage, bacon, eggs, beans, fried bread, mushrooms, and grilled tomatoes arrived with a pot of tea for each man.

Rex licked his lips and stared at the plates, focusing his effort on Dobbs – he looked like an easy mark.

Dobbs paused with his fork hand halfway to his mouth when he spotted Rex's wide, imploring eyes.

'Is he hungry?' he asked, looking at Rex the whole time.

Albert looked up from his own breakfast and tutted.

'No, he isn't. Rex, lie down.'

Rex made a grumpy face.

The humans could hear his loud grumbling as he settled to the carpet. 'Stupid humans and their stupid tasty food. I am hungry, I'll have you know. My stomach got reset to zero last night and that meagre bowl of breakfast kibble did not refill it.'

Acknowledging that Rex was going to continue making grumpy noises until he got something to eat, Albert cut off a chunk of sausage and slipped it under the table. It was that or have to ignore the disapproving looks of other guests in the hotel's restaurant or abandon his breakfast to return Rex to the room. Losing half a sausage was easier.

Rex mumbled, 'Rank roo,' around the mouthful of hot sausage, rolling it around his mouth until the greasy finger of pork cooled down enough to eat.

Bellies satisfied, two men and a dog left the hotel just after ten o'clock on a mission to solve a murder.

'Where are we going first?' Dobbs wanted to know.

Albert waved to a passing taxi, getting the driver's attention as he gave a cryptic response, 'We are going back in time.'

Albert's plan, much to Dobbs' disappointment did not involve a DeLorean time machine, but a trip to the local public library where they visited the research and archive wing.

If there was one thing Albert knew, it was how to find historic information.

'I want to know what school Danny Parsons went to,' he explained. 'His mother, Pauline, hinted that there was something in the past that linked him to Chris Caan. My daughter, a serving senior detective, did some digging for me last night and was able to turn up that Chris Caan went to catering college with Jack Marley.'

'Really, wow,' commented Dobbs. 'I don't think anyone else knows that.'

'They will,' Albert promised. 'DI Brownlow is no slouch so she will find that connection.'

'So why are we bothering?'

Albert rolled his eyes. 'Because she will assume it reinforces her belief that Jack killed Chris.'

'And you still think he didn't,' Dobbs concluded.

Rather than answer, Albert stepped up to the librarian lady sitting behind a large, polished desk. She raised an index finger to beg a moment's grace; she wanted to finish the task she had at hand.

Dobbs nudged Albert's arm.

'If you want to know what school Danny went to, it's right here on the internet.'

Albert twisted his head around. 'It is?'

Dobbs watched the old man's face for a few seconds, waiting for a punchline. When it didn't come, he said, 'Of course. Everything is on the internet.' He held the phone in front of Albert's face so he could see. 'Look, it's on his social media profile. He went to St Jude's Catholic School, that would be until he was eleven, I guess. Then he went to Harper Grammar. How about that? We went to the same school.'

Dobbs was remarking about a minor coincidence while Albert marvelled at what could be done with a phone. He didn't have his reading glasses on, so couldn't actually see what the phone displayed. There was, however, no reason to doubt what he was being told.

Lying on the hardwearing library carpet, Rex was bored. He had been in libraries a few times and there was nothing in them to interest him. Humans did this weird thing with books where they would stare for hours, barely moving and rarely speaking.

Rex didn't mind that too much because when his human did it, he could generally lie on the sofa and go to sleep with his head on the old man's lap. Otherwise, it was a boring enterprise he could make no sense of.

Also, libraries didn't smell of anything other than musty, old bits of paper. Closing his eyes, he thought about Mrs Caan again. When they left their room this morning, there had been no scent in the air to indicate she was around. The same had been true last night, which made him question where she had gotten to.

His human, given enough time to figure things out, usually arrived at the right conclusion. This time, though, Rex was starting to think he might need more help than usual. The dead man's wife was to blame, he was certain of it, but here they were at a library.

If his human didn't figure it out soon, Rex was going to have to go looking for her himself.

Above the snoozing hound's head, Dobbs showed Albert that Jack Marley also attended St Jude's. Not only was he in the same school as Danny Parsons, the two men were in the same class. There was a photograph showing their graduating year, the two eighteen-year-olds easy to spot because the clever software embedded in the social media site identified them.

The librarian lady finished what she was doing and looked up.

'My apologies, gentlemen. Thank you for your patien ...' her words trailed off as she saw the two men and the dog going back out the doors.

'So we are going to St Jude's?' Dobbs sought confirmation.

Albert waggled his eyebrows again. 'Not yet.'

Unexpected Visitors and Chocolate Challenges

Albert had a mental map of Clitheroe stored in his head. Even so, he wasn't sure where the hospital was in relation to anything else. They were at the library which placed them most of a mile from the hotel. He wanted to visit the hospital next, but he couldn't take Rex with him, and he didn't want to walk back to their hotel only to find the hospital was in the opposite direction.

'That's all right,' smiled Dobbs, 'we can just take my car. It's at the hotel.'

Albert sucked on his top lip as he considered finding a house brick to thump on Dobbs' head.

'Why did I just pay twenty quid for a taxi to get to the library when your car is at the hotel?'

Dobbs just gaped open-mouthed.

'You never said anything. I thought you wanted to get a taxi.'

'Why … no, never mind.' Albert dismissed the argument before it could brew. 'Let's get your car then, shall we?'

It took all of twelve minutes to cross Clitheroe again, Rex leading the way and stopping here and there to sniff interesting smells. They walked through a park which gave Albert the chance to let Rex off his lead. It added a couple of minutes but was of no concern. They arrived back at the hotel soon enough where Albert discovered Dobbs had first called him after stepping out of his car just twenty yards from the hotel's front door.

He felt like rolling his eyes again, but resisted, focusing on the car instead.

Dobbs drove a fifteen-year-old Toyota Rav4. A blue one. Its bodywork had seen better days, the tyres were almost bald, there was a crack in the windscreen and the driver's door mirror was missing.

'Is this thing even road legal?' he asked, certain it could not be.

Dobbs sniggered. 'That's one of the best things about being a police officer. You get to know all the bent blokes. I get a pass on my inspection without even having to take it to the shop.'

If Albert had false teeth, that would have been the point where he spat them out.

'You're not joking, are you?' Albert blurted. 'My God, man, have you no integrity?'

Dobbs' happy expression fell away. He was being admonished, which happened a lot, but he wasn't sure what for.

'You are supposed to be above reproach. You are supposed to bring the bent blokes to justice, shutting them down so they don't let dangerous vehicles onto the road. How can you expect to uphold the laws of this land if you don't adhere to them yourself?'

Dobbs tried to fumble his way to a response of some kind. One that would answer the old man's questions while not sounding like a total idiot. 'Well, um. It's just that.'

Albert held his hand up to Dobbs' face and muttered obscenities under his breath with his eyes closed and his attention on a hopeful spot residing in the kindly part of his soul.

Rex widdled on the driver's side front tyre. He needed a place to go, and it was to hand.

Albert glanced down at his dog.

'Well said, Rex.'

Hoping to move the conversation along, Dobbs plipped the car open.

'Shall we go?'

Albert felt like banging Dobbs' head on the car to see if he could knock some sense into it. The right thing to do would be to get another taxi but having a car at his disposal meant for faster movement when he wanted to go somewhere, and he could take Rex with him.

Sighing loudly at his lack of choices, Albert walked around the car to get in the other side.

'Come along, Rex. Just cross your toes and hope it doesn't explode or something.'

It turned out that Albert's concern for the car's serviceability were unfounded. Aside from the missing door mirror, the car sounded and operated as if it were in good condition. It was even tidy inside.

With the backseats folded flat, Rex had plenty of space to stretch out. He did just that, sliding his front paws way out in front before laying his jaw on them. When Albert next checked him, the dog appeared to be asleep.

Rex's eyes were closed, but he was still alert, and his nose was working overtime. There was food in the car. The first item he detected was a piece of kebab meat. It was under the driver's seat where Dobbs dropped it three days ago, eating while driving on his way home from a late shift. A half-eaten chocolate bar was in the driver's door bin and Rex could smell something else, but he wasn't yet sure what it might be.

It was sweet, that was for certain; Rex could smell the sticky sugary goodness.

There was no good in attempting to find any of it while his human was in the car, so Rex rested his eyes and daydreamed about what he might find if the humans were foolish enough to leave him unguarded at any point.

That happened sooner than expected.

At the hospital, Dobbs angled his car toward the disabled spaces right next to the accident and emergency entrance. They were the ones closest to the buildings and he had a purloined disabled badge to put in his window – one he'd confiscated more than a year ago from someone parking in the spaces when they ought not to be.

Only at the last second did he veer off. Given Albert's demeanour toward cops bending the rules, he doubted the old man would approve even if it would save them a walk.

Albert had been about to question what Dobbs thought he was doing. When he changed course, swinging away from the disabled space, Albert frowned for a second, then rudely opened the glove box.

Dobbs said nothing when his passenger held up the blue disabled parking badge with a raised eyebrow. He also kept his lips tightly sealed when Albert put the badge into his coat pocket.

Finding a parking space required circling the carpark twice. Dobbs thought about making a comment since the disabled spots were all free, but a set of reverse lights ahead as a car manoeuvred from a space stopped him.

Albert twisted in his seat to say, 'You need to stay here, Rex.'

The dog had got back into a sitting position to look around in anticipation that they were all getting out. The news that he was staying put didn't bother him at all. He was going to explore the car.

With the windows wound down two inches, and the cool late autumn air flowing through, Albert held no concern for Rex's safety or health. He didn't plan to be long anyway.

Rex got a pat on the head and a ruffle of his fur, before watching intently until the humans were out of sight. The second that happened, he dived into the front seat and started to snuffle for the source of the food smells.

Fifty yards away, Albert's feet had stopped dead.

He was staring at a car. Dobbs, still jabbering nonsense about beer and/or football - Albert hadn't been listening, failed to notice the old man was no longer with him. He got ten yards before he glanced to his left and found only empty space.

Albert was behind him, staring at a vintage Bentley. He saw why when he backtracked.

The license plate was one of those people paid good money for; a private plate where the number and letter combination could be tortured to spell out a word.

This one read: C4ANS.

'Why is Mrs Caan at the hospital?' Albert asked the air. He didn't know it was Emelia Caan's car but was willing to bet his pension that it had to be.

'Maybe she knows someone here?' suggested Dobbs, failing to realise the question had been rhetorical. Albert wanted an answer but hadn't expected Dobbs to supply one.

Albert picked at his chin, scratching it absentmindedly. Why on earth was Mrs Caan here? What else did he not know?

Rex would have answered his question, but he was trying to force his snout to the bottom of the driver's door bin. It was wedging just before he could get to the chocolate bar lying at the bottom. If he pushed his tongue out between his teeth, he could just about lick the top of the chocolate bar. It was tantalisingly close, but try as he might, he could not get to it.

He reversed out and tried a different angle.

What he needed was a sidekick dog to help. Someone with a smaller face, like Hans from Biggleswade for instance. Hans would be able to get it and they could then share the prize. Half of half of a half-eaten chocolate bar was still vastly superior to all of a treat he couldn't reach.

Albert strolled through the hospital's main entrance, the automatic doors swishing open to let him in. Dobbs was by the old man's shoulder.

They went directly to the reception desk where Albert asked if Mrs Emelia Caan was registered on their system as a visitor for any reason. It drew a total blank, the computer having no record of her. To Albert, that meant she had to be here visiting someone. Quite who that might be he couldn't guess.

They passed squad cars on their way in. Their presence hadn't really registered in Albert's head, and he would have ignored them if Dobbs hadn't pointed out the vintage Jaguar parked right by them – it belonged to DI Brownlow. She regularly used her own transport apparently, one of those officers who chose style over money because the reimbursement available was pitiful compared to the running costs.

Her presence, given that Albert believed she was trying to keep him shut out of the investigation, complicated things. Albert expected to find Pauline and Matilda by Danny's bedside. Where else would they be? However, if DI Brownlow was here, his guess was that Danny was now awake and talking. She was here to tie up some loose ends and get to the bottom of why Jack Marley stabbed him.

Dobbs tapped Albert on the arm, getting his attention.

'I don't think she will like that I am here, Albert. Maybe I should wait in the car?'

'I'm not planning to let her see us,' Albert replied, not breaking his stride as they made their way through the hospital.

'There's likely to be a guard on the door.'

Dobbs' second comment gave Albert cause to slow his pace. It was only momentary though. If there was an officer on the door, he wouldn't be there to keep Albert out, though that might be a secondary task if DI Brownlow was feeling particularly paranoid. Rather, the officer would be there as a statement of the police interest in Danny Parsons. He was a victim and a witness. His testimony, depending on what he knew, might be enough to put Jack Marley away for murder.

Inspired by his initial success posing as a Food Health agent, Albert was going to try the same trick here if he needed to. Okay, so dressing as a doctor in a hospital is a ridiculous cliché, he admitted silently to himself, but that's no reason why it won't work.

The doctors going by were dressed in smart trousers and oxford shirts. It was a uniform of sorts even if they were all wearing their own clothes. He was older than those he saw, by several decades in many cases, but he saw one gentleman in his sixties with an entourage of junior physicians trailing in his wake. He was talking and they were all trying not only to keep up but to answer his questions at the same time.

A quick study of the senior doctor's mannerisms instilled in Albert a belief that, provided he was unchallenged by a medical professional, he could get in to see the Parsons family. He only needed to bluff one cop at the most.

What he needed to find was a couple of props.

In the car, Rex had finally worked out how to use a front paw to sweep the chocolate bar along the door bin. The trick was to get it moving fast enough that it popped up when it got to the end and then shift his body swiftly enough to catch it with his teeth before it fell back down again.

There was barely enough room for his body under the steering wheel, and if he stood on the driver's seat, his angles were all too awkward. He tried turning around. However, manoeuvring in the tight space, his back left paw got caught on something. It was looped behind a handle or something. It didn't hurt but he was off balance on the spongey seat and unable to turn his head the right way to see how to extricate the trapped limb.

Frustrated, he gave it a yank and the door popped open.

Shocked at the change in circumstances, Rex put his rescued paw down and nudged the door with his head.

What had he done? He frowned at the door, staring at the different components, and wondering which one of them had set him free. It mattered not, he decided, dropping down to the ground outside.

He was free to roam, but he didn't want to go anywhere, there was still a chocolate bar right there if he could get to it. His nose then reminded him that the chocolate bar wasn't the only treat to be had. Now that he was at ground level, he could see under the driver's seat and didn't even need his nose to find the stray piece of kebab meat.

It was chewy, not that he chewed it, and covered in fluff, not that he cared. The succulent morsel vanished never to return a half second after Rex got his teeth on it. Swallowing, he turned his attention to the other thing he could smell.

The sweet thing.

He didn't know what it was, but he could tell it was food. Or, rather, it was drink.

Tucked down behind the driver's seat was a can of something. The smell was coming from spilled liquid coating the tin of drink. Two days ago, when Dobbs tipped his head back to take a sip, he'd almost lost control of his car. Half the can in his hand had gone over Dobbs' lap and the second can he had trapped between his thighs.

Rex licked it, his tongue reacting as if the sticky, congealed liquid were electric. He darted back a pace, moving his tongue around and questioning what he might have found. The silver and blue can with its brightly coloured bull logo meant nothing to him.

It was difficult to get to where it was, so he craned his head through the gap to get it behind the seat and bit hold of the can to extract it. Once out of the car, he could get a better look.

However, as he tugged, one of his teeth made a tiny puncture hole and the pressurised liquid inside exploded into his mouth, it made him jump. However, describing his reaction as jumping is to fail to give colour to the event.

To a witness, the sight were as if a wasp had just stung the dog's wotsits. Rex reared upward like a startled horse, spitting the can from his mouth as an arc of liquid shot through the sky.

Rex banged into the car parked next to the Rav4, rocking its suspension, and he barked in shock. Poised to start running away from the insane can and its deadly contents, Rex realised he rather liked the taste. He licked his lips, familiarising himself with the odd flavour. The same electric feeling resulted. Whatever this stuff was, it was good.

While inside the hospital, his human 'borrowed' a set of scrubs and a stethoscope from a nurses' station, Rex got on with licking up all the strange liquid.

Fooling No One

'We're not going to fool anyone.'

Albert took a step back to inspect Dobbs while the constable voiced his concerns for the third or fourth time. Dobbs needed a disguise that hid his face because the cop standing outside Danny Parsons' room knew him. That's why he was now wearing a set of green surgical scrubs and a facemask.

They were crammed inside a toilet where Albert insisted Dobbs shed his jeans and coat to don the doctor's outfit. The biggest problem was that the scrubs didn't exactly fit. Dobbs was tall and wide, and the scrubs were not. The sleeves ended four inches before they reached his wrists, and the legs didn't make it to his ankles.

'I look ridiculous,' he whined, checking his reflection in the mirror.

Albert, in contrast, unless a person was to consider that he looked old still to be practicing medicine, looked very much the part. His reading glasses became another prop – one which helped to change the shape of his face, and the stethoscope around his neck made him look like all the other senior physicians.

'Look,' he tried to coax Dobbs into playing along. 'All we have to do is bluff our way past one guard. I'll do all the talking. He probably won't even look at you.'

'What if he asks to see our identification?' Dobbs threw out another barrier to their success.

Albert grinned. 'I'll use a Jedi mind trick on him.' Then he mimed using his right index finger as he said, 'You don't need to see our identification.'

In Albert's opinion, his Alec Guinness impersonation was a good one. Dobbs' face suggested otherwise.

'Seriously though?' Dobbs wanted a proper answer.

Albert grabbed for the toilet door handle. He was going anyway. 'If he asks to see our ID, we act like we can't find it, say we must have left it in the locker room, and make like we are going back for it. If we can't get in to see Danny, so be it. I am at least going to try.'

Without another word, he pushed the door open and started towards Danny Parsons' room.

Around the corner, they found the cop looking bored and scratching his backside. He stopped when he realised someone was coming and straightened himself up.

Albert paid the man no attention, putting on his best doctor's act and talking to Dobbs as they made their way along the corridor.

'Yes, it was a trans-sectional inverse contusion of the liver. When we biopsied it, we found carcinomatous tissue growing. The surgery was one of the most complicated I have ever led. I have to give a lecture on liver resection tomorrow if you are free.'

He continued to babble utter nonsense right up until they got to the cop. At the last moment, Albert switched his attention to meet the uniformed officer's gaze.

'Doctors Frome and Hawkins to see Mr Parsons. Is he alone?' Albert didn't break stride, expecting the cop to step aside, and intending to walk straight in.

The police officer grinned.

'Wotcha, Dobbsy. What are you doing dressed up like that?'

Dobbs groaned loudly and tore off his face mask.

'I told you this wouldn't work.' Meeting the questioning expression of his colleague, he said, 'Look, Bazza, I need to ask last night's stab victim a few questions. Can you let us in?'

The cop raised his eyebrows, but said, 'Sure.' Reaching for the door handle, he swung the door open and stepped to his right so they could enter.

Albert looked down at his clothes and stethoscope, and then back up at the police officer. He was frowning.

'Do I not look like a doctor?'

Bazza pulled a face. 'Well, sort of, I guess. Except ...'

'Yes,' Albert encouraged even though he doubted he would like what the man was about to say.

'Well, you're a bit old.'

Albert harrumphed as he went through the door and into the private hospital room. Too concerned with his failure to pull off his attempt at subterfuge, he failed to consider who else might be in the room.

'You!' screeched Pauline.

Albert froze. 'Oh, bother.'

Danny's mother was already crossing the room, her hands coming up as if she planned to physically attack him.

Hearing a shout from inside the room, Constable Barry 'Bazza' Douthwaite burst through the door. Guarding a bloke asleep in his hospital bed while his attacker was in custody and thus the likelihood of there being anything to do had not been Barry's first choice of assignment today. However, it was in the warm and he'd already been able to chat up four different nurses, securing one of their numbers to call later.

Now his quiet duty was going sideways, and he knew DI Brownlow was in the building somewhere. She'd already been in to see Danny Parsons, and she was coming back. She only left to give the man some time to consider his story. If she came back and found bedlam occurring, he would be in for it.

Arriving in the private room, he unintentionally placed himself in between the old man and Danny's mother. Consequently, he caught the slap she was aiming at Albert's head.

'Gran!' squealed Matilda. She was on the other side of the bed, holding her dad's hand.

'What's he doing here?' demanded Pauline. Unconcerned that she had just struck a police officer, she was now trying to shove her way around him to get to Albert as he retreated another pace.

Albert protested, 'I am here to help.'

His words fell on deaf ears but Barry, recovering quickly from the slap which startled him rather than hurt, made sure Pauline stayed where she was.

'Mrs Parsons,' he raised his voice to get her attention. 'You will kindly desist.'

When all parties were silent for a beat, Constable Douthwaite asked, 'Right, now someone tell me what is going on here.'

Pauline jumped in first, an accusing finger jabbing the air as she glared at Albert.

'He was in our restaurant yesterday pretending to be from the Food Health Governing Body. He stole hotpots from our kitchen and ran off when the real Food Health agents turned up. I want to know what his game is.'

Constable Douthwaite had not expected this. To his ears, it sounded like the old man might be involved in the mystery surrounding the death of Chris Caan and the subsequent stabbing of the restaurant owner he was now guarding. DI Brownlow was leading the investigation, but maybe there were some points to be scored. Did she know about the old man?

'Is that true?' he asked, reaching to the set of cuffs on his belt. He didn't remove them yet, but the gesture did not go unnoticed.

'Go on, cuff 'im,' encouraged Pauline, her eyes shining with excitement.

Albert met the officer's eyes. 'It is true,' he admitted with no shame. 'I am investigating the same case. I am a retired detective superintendent. Your colleague, Constable Dobbs, is helping me.' He turned his attention to Danny Parsons.

The restaurant owner was lying in bed and looking a little drugged. Albert assumed he had been given painkiller medication, but though he was yet to speak, his eyes were open, and he raised his eyebrows when Albert looked his way.

'I apologise for the subterfuge at your restaurant. At the time I thought it was necessary.'

Matilda asked, 'Is that why you were asking so many questions that were not about the food?'

'Who cares?' raged Pauline, unwilling to let Albert off the hook. 'He stole two hotpots and that makes him a criminal.'

Keeping his attention on the man in the bed, Albert explained, 'I came to Clitheroe for your hotpot, Mr Parsons. You have won the awards and I wanted to taste it. Initially, my motivation for solving the mystery of Chris Caan's death was purely selfish – I needed to find who was to blame so I could clear your name and that of your restaurant in order that I might dine there. That's not going to happen though, is it, Mr Parsons? What did you put in the hotpots?'

Still the other side of Constable Douthwaite, Pauline exploded.

'What! How dare you? Danny had nothing to do with what happened to Chris Caan! He would never ...'

Shouting to be heard over her screeching, Albert said, 'I am trying to help, Danny. The truth will come out. It always does. You knew Jack Marley and you knew Chris Caan. What is the connection, Danny? Why did Jack Marley attack you last night?'

Constable Douthwaite felt that the situation had escaped him. He was supposed to be in control and that meant he ought to kick the old man out. What if he was onto something though? Dobbsy was working with him; that had to mean something, and he said he used to be a very senior detective.

Hoping he might be about to hear a vital clue, he chose to wait to hear what the stab victim might have to say.

All eyes were on Danny. All except Pauline's, who was eyeing the cuffs on the back of Constable Douthwaite's belt. She wondered what he would do if she decided to use them to perform a citizens' arrest on the old man. In her opinion he was clearly mad and therefore arguably a danger to himself and all those around him.

No one was watching the door, which is why none of them saw it opening.

Rex felt odd. His brain felt sparkly, like there was electricity zipping through it and his body had a sort of supercharged feel to it. His heart was beating faster than normal - he could tell without needing to feel his pulse, and everything around him had a kind of slow-motion effect to it.

He wanted to chase something. His muscles were coiled springs waiting to be released. Whatever was in the strange silver and blue can had magical properties.

The click, click of high heels on tarmac reached his ears, bringing his head around and his nose up. Like an uppercut to his olfactory system, a scent he knew hit him and it propelled him out from between the cars to land in the open space of the carpark.

Emelia Caan froze.

The dog was looking right at her. Was it the same one from the hotel? Surely it couldn't be. She wanted to dismiss the notion – there had to be dozens or even hundreds of German Shepherds in Clitheroe – but the dog looked just like the one that forced its way into her room yesterday, and it was staring right at her.

'Shoo,' she urged, waving her arm to make Rex go away.

They were thirty yards apart and she was about eight yards from her car. She had the keys in her hand.

Rex growled.

'I know what you did. My human will figure it out eventually, but if I present you to him, maybe he will get there sooner. Since I know you are guilty,' Rex bared his teeth, 'how about a game of chase and bite?'

Emelia squealed in fright, her eyes going as wide as saucers when the dog snarled and broke into a run.

Her car was right there, and it was already open, but she could tell there was no chance she could get to it before the dog got to her.

The question about whether this was the same dog from her hotel room was unanswered but also now of minor concern. The dog was coming for her, and she needed to be elsewhere.

Dropping her bag as she screamed for help and started running, her brain ran a few quick calculations to return an answer she did not wish to hear – there was no one in sight and nowhere for her to hide.

Under any other set of circumstances, Rex would have never chased the woman. He believed with absolute certainty that she was behind the murder, but even so, chasing and biting without the command to do so was strictly in the 'bad dog' camp of behaviour.

His brain, however, was not firing in its usual manner. Hopped up on caffeine, he felt wired. He was ready to wrestle crocodiles and fight bears. If a T-Rex had wandered into the carpark, Rex would have kicked it in the wotsits and asked if it thought it was tough enough to beat him.

He felt strong. He felt alive.

He threw up.

The strange tasting liquid, whatever the heck it was, did not agree with him. But undeterred, he leapt over the pool of his own vomit, and barking like a dog possessed, for the caffeine was in his bloodstream now, he got back to the task of chasing Emelia Caan.

'Help!' she screamed, twisting her head as she ran, then screaming again even louder because the dog was ten yards closer than it had been the last time she looked. 'Help!'

Fuelled by blind panic, certain she couldn't outrun the dog, and looking for any direction that might offer the slightest hope of refuge from the hell hound on her heels, she did something she had never once done in her life and climbed a car.

As tactics go, it was fairly lame.

Rex saw his quarry leap onto the bonnet of a Volvo and matched her move. With the cars parked so close together, once he landed on the French car closest to him, he could simply run from one to the next.

And that was exactly what he did.

The sound of the flimsy metal panels deforming and then resetting as the dog leapt from car to car reached Emelia's ears.

'Arrrrrghhhh!'

Her cry of terror merely spurred Rex onward. He was going to be on her in two seconds.

Tripping over her own feet and falling backward, her hand went through free space when her brain was convinced it should have found the car's roof. It kept going until her ribs slammed into the top edge of the windscreen and then she saw it.

The sunroof was open!

Quite why anyone would have an open hole in the roof of their car on such a cold day she could not fathom. Nor could she afford to stay where she was and question it.

Rex hit the next but last car, barking his excitement one last time. One more bound was all that stood between him and a chase and bite victory. So imagine his surprise when the woman vanished before his eyes.

Momentarily stunned, Rex skidded to a halt. The question of where she had gone resolved itself a heartbeat later when she popped up inside the car. His canine brain didn't think to jump onto the car's roof. Had it done so, he would have found the open aperture just in time for Emelia to shove the umbrella she found inside up his nose.

The answer to her question about the sunroof was that the mechanism was broken. Emelia found that out when she grabbed the handle – amazed at her luck in finding a car so old it had a manual winder – that the whole thing was jammed.

Rex was incensed. Hiding inside a car was cheating. He barked raucously, venting his frustration. He could see Emelia, but how to get to her? He bit hold of a windscreen wiper simply because it was there. When a tug ripped it away from the window, he let it go again but by then it was mangled and stuck out from the car at an odd angle. He tried the other one, this time keeping hold of it and shaking his whole body in an attempt to tear it loose.

Defeated, he spat it out, barked again, then jumped down to see if there was another way into the car.

He bit the plastic front grill which promptly chose to play dead, falling to the ground with a clatter.

Emelia, gasping to get air into her lungs, felt each shake of the car. She was safe, for now at least she told herself, but she still needed to get away from the dog. Scanning around, she could see no one coming to her rescue. All her screaming had attracted the sum total of zero people.

How on earth had the dog timed its attack for the one patch of time when there was no one coming or going from the hospital carpark?

Could she hotwire the car? Could she do that? Staring at the steering wheel bezel and the cables she could see running out of the bottom, she pulled a face – her knowledge of electrics was on par with her knowledge of nuclear physics – she knew nothing about either.

The sound of something else being torn from the front end of the car got her attention, and it was in that moment that she realised how dumb she was being.

The sound of the horn suddenly blaring made Rex jump backwards. His fear was momentary though and born only of shock because the car's horn was located right there next to his face. Tearing the front grill off had exposed it.

Looking up at the windscreen, he could see the woman inside making a face at him as she mashed her left hand against the centre of the steering wheel and made a strange gesture with the middle finger of her right hand.

Rex had no idea what the hand signal was supposed to tell him, but he knew what to do about the noise assailing his ears.

When the horn abruptly stopped working, Emelia took her hand away from the button and tried again. People would hear the horn and would come looking. Why was it not working?

She got her answer when Rex lifted his head above the level of the bonnet. The horn was between his teeth. He spat it out.

Emelia screamed again, but the few seconds the horn had sounded was enough to do the trick; a pair of ambulance drivers could see Rex, and though they could not yet see the woman trapped in the already part-dismantled Volvo, they were on their way to investigate.

The Low Point

'What on earth is happening here?' roared DI Brownlow.

Bazza cringed. Dobbs put his facemask back on and tried to make himself invisible. Pauline whipped around to start screaming for the senior officer to do something about the intruders in her son's hospital room, but Albert got there first.

'Jack Marley didn't kill Chris Caan.'

The detective inspector filled the doorway, not that she was a big woman, far from it, but the magnitude of her attitude made her seem fifty percent bigger.

'Douthwaite, I gave you a very simple task and yet you have failed to perform it.' That she addressed her officer and ignored Albert told him volumes.

'You're not going to listen, are you?' Albert accused her.

Constable Douthwaite was already moving to get Albert. He was reaching for the old man's arm, intending to escort him swiftly from the room. He didn't need to be removed; Albert would take himself without the need for further instruction, but DI Brownlow chose to respond to his latest question.

'This is a police investigation, Mr Smith. Do you think I don't know about your children pulling files? I have recorded a complaint against your daughter already. It is one thing to take an interest, and another entirely to share confidential information with a civilian. That is what you are, Mr Smith. Do you understand that?'

Albert smiled at her with kindly eyes. 'Jack Marley did not kill Chris Caan,' he repeated. 'You are going to find sufficient evidence to convict him, and I suspect that he is a troubled individual who should, for the safety of everyone else, be locked away until rehabilitated. However, he is not guilty of murder.'

DI Brownlow humoured the old man. 'You have irrefutable evidence to present, Mr Smith?'

Albert's smile widened. 'Not one tiny bit.'

The smile on the old man's face was disconcerting but it was the admission she'd been after, so she grasped it.

'Because none exists, Mr Smith. My own investigation revealed a connection between Chris Caan and Jack Marley. They attended catering college together but where Chris Caan went on to achieve fame and fortune, Jack Marley ran a small restaurant that was on the cusp of failing. He begged an old friend to help him with an endorsement, but Chris Caan chose to provide an honest assessment of the food Jack Marley sold. It ruined him, and for that Jack Marley killed Chris Caan.' Dismissing Albert, she turned her attention to Danny Parsons.

He was still in his bed and still holding Matilda's hand. However, to Albert, the biggest point to note was how tight lipped the man was being. He was yet to say a word.

'Now, Mr Parsons, perhaps we can get back to our interview,' her tone was soft and caring – she was talking to a victim now. 'I need to know why Jack Marley attacked you last night. If you were being coerced or blackmailed now is the time to admit it.' Without looking up from Danny's face, she growled, 'Douthwaite why is Mr Smith still in here?'

Spurred into action, Constable Douthwaite held out his right arm to guide Albert from the room.

'Sir,' he uttered one word with enough meaning to convey the DI's wishes.

Dobbs chose that moment to attempt his escape. So far, Brownlow hadn't once looked at him. His statue-like stillness had made him almost invisible. Moving ruined it.

'Stop!' barked DI Brownlow, her eye refusing to believe what they could see. 'Dobbs! Dobbs what ...' She lunged for his face, ripping the mask off. 'This is the last straw. What are you doing here? Are you helping the old man? You're finished this time, Dobbs. I wouldn't even bother ironing your uniform again. Get out.' She spat the final command at him.

It was a horrible scene to witness. He was a rubbish police officer, and he had probably been annoying Brownlow with his laziness and ineptitude for years. Even so, Albert felt bad for the part he had played in bringing things to a head. If the man were to lose his job now, Albert would have to accept some of the blame.

It ended his desire to throw one last retort on his way out the door. Silently, he let Constable Douthwaite guide him from the room, Dobbs following close behind.

Before they arrived in the hallway outside, the detective inspector was apologising to the Parsons family.

'I'm sorry you had to see that. Please do not allow the poor judgement and performance of two junior officers cloud your opinion of local law enforcement. Now, Mr Parsons, I know you were not involved in the murder of Chris Caan, but I do know that you went to school with Jack Marley.'

Albert strained his ears to hear what was being said but when Douthwaite closed the door with all three of them back in the corridor outside, any chance to eavesdrop was denied.

Dobbs looked miserable. His eyes were cast down to the tiled floor and his whole body was sagging.

Albert felt it necessary to say something.

'I'm sorry, Dobbs. DI Brownlow has it wrong. I shall make sure your chief constable hears an accurate report of your efforts.'

'It won't make any difference,' Dobbs mumbled. 'The chief constable thinks I'm an idiot too.'

'Then we must solve this case, Dobbs. If we prove that Jack Marley is innocent, we can show that your means, while controversial, were necessary to avoid a miscarriage of justice.'

Dobbs raised his head, meeting Albert's eyes.

'If it's all the same to you. I think I'll just go to the pub. I'd like to drown my sorrows.'

Albert shook his head vigorously. 'No, Dobbs. I think I might have this worked out. We just need to check a few things. There is a missing part to this puzzle and all we have to do is find it. You'll see.'

Dobbs had no interest in pursuing the old man's daft investigation any further. It had sucked up good drinking time already and done nothing but lose him his job. He would get a disciplinary meeting in a few days' time, but he doubted even a union rep could do anything to change the inevitable outcome.

He did not get to voice his thoughts because the sound of shouting interrupted them.

Constable Douthwaite, back in front of the door he was supposed to be guarding, leaned forward to stare down the corridor.

'What the devil?'

People were squealing and screaming in fright and diving out of the way as they tried to avoid something the three men outside Danny Parsons' room couldn't see. Patients and hospital staff alike were hugging the walls of the corridor or ducking into doorways to get out of the way of something.

It was coming their way, it was moving fast, and there were half a dozen men in hospital security uniforms chasing it.

Albert got a sinking feeling in his stomach.

It trebled a second later when he heard a bark. He recognised the voice behind it.

Rex had attempted to reason with the humans who came to rescue the woman in the car. She was a bad person and they needed to get his human because the old man would understand why Rex had her pinned where she couldn't escape.

The humans were not listening though. They were getting very excited about the barking dog who they took to be aggressive and dangerous.

Emelia Caan screamed blue murder the moment the first people started to arrive. The two ambulance drivers quickly called for help when the dog refused to calm down. Two onsite security guards turned up within a minute and they immediately called for backup.

It didn't help Rex's case that he had trashed the Volvo as he vented his rage.

The reinforcements brought blankets with which they began to corral the dog. Forcing him back and away from the car, they were able to get the trapped and visibly shaken woman out.

Now incensed to the point of being apoplectic, Rex couldn't get to the guilty woman and was being forced farther and farther away from her. When his retreating back paw stepped on something, he looked down to find it was Emelia Caan's handbag. Flashing his head around to look at it, he saw the bottle of pills again.

As the security guards attempted to surround him – their plan was to throw the blankets over the giant, mad dog to trap him - Rex scooped the pill bottle in his mouth, leapt on the bonnet of a handy Mercedes, ran over the roof, and shot off toward the hospital entrance.

Inside, he had to follow his nose, which was nigh on impossible with so many people and so many other scents, but dashing down a corridor he caught his human's scent and there ahead of him was the old man. He looked bewildered and not entirely pleased to see his dog.

Rex applied the brakes, sliding a little on the tiles when his claws found too little purchase. Arriving at his human's feet, he wagged his tail and spat the pill bottle onto the floor.

'Here. The woman did it. The dead man's mate. I'm not sure what is in this bottle, but she's been lying about stuff since we arrived. I'm pretty sure you're going to find out she poisoned him with these. So, well, here you go, case solved. You can thank me later. Right now, I think perhaps I ought to keep running.'

The security guards, out of breath, unused to running, and doing their best to catch up to the dog while avoiding patients and such, were ten yards away now and three seconds from catching up to their target.

Rex bunched his leg muscles to launch himself into another sprint. This had been fun. It was kind of like a game of chase and bite but in reverse.

Albert hooked a hand through his collar.

'Is ... this ... your ... dog ... sir?' asked the first security guard to arrive. He could barely speak he was so out of breath and had to be ten years younger and thirty pounds lighter than most of his colleagues.

Cringing, Albert said, 'Yes. Is there a problem?'

Follow That Car

Getting out of the hospital took over an hour. Rex was completely calm the whole time, which ruined the guards' claims that he was dangerous, possibly rabid, and needed to be destroyed for the safety of the human population. The fact of it was that Rex was coming down off a massive sugar high and wanted to do nothing but sleep. He felt utterly spent, but the net result was his relaxed, sleepy state made the guards look foolish.

They protested that he had cornered a woman in a car, but the lady in question had left the moment the guards chased Rex toward the hospital. Without her testimony it came down to their report of the dog destroying a car, but when they went back to the parking space, the Volvo was gone.

Whether the owner had noticed the missing parts and mangled windscreen wipers or not was moot. They did find the car's plastic front grill, but it hardly constituted hard evidence. No one on the security team thought to note the car's registration plate which left little hope of ever working out who it belonged too.

That the dog had ventured inside the hospital broke a bunch of protocols, but it wasn't as if the dog could be held accountable.

Albert got a stern warning from the head of hospital administration - a sharply dressed woman in her late thirties. Her concern though was all to do with leaving dogs in cars in the first place since that was what Albert claimed to have done.

More than anything, the incident had highlighted inadequacies in the security team's training.

Albert left the administration lady to deal with that matter as she saw fit and left the hospital using the belt from a hospital robe as a lead since Rex's was still in Dobbs' car.

Dobbs had vanished during the initial dog chase incident. Albert didn't see him go; he just turned around to say something to him only to discover empty air where the constable had previously been standing.

His car was gone too, Albert found which was a little disappointing since Rex's lead was still in it.

He looked down at Rex, getting a tail wag in response.

'You probably don't need any exercise, do you?'

Rex was feeling more like his old self, the highs and lows of laxatives and energy drinks notwithstanding, but given a choice, he would spend his afternoon asleep on a rug somewhere.

There were taxis by the hospital entrance. Albert hopped in the one at the head of the queue.

'Where to, sir?' asked the driver, twisting in his seat to look at his customer.

Albert was about to answer when he spotted someone exiting through the hospital's main entrance. It was Matilda, Danny Parsons' daughter and she was moving swiftly. She had somewhere to go that was more important than staying with her dad.

'Um,' Albert sucked on his teeth as he watched her cross the carpark. 'This might sound like an odd request, but I need you to follow someone.'

The taxi driver frowned, thought about refusing because it sounded like a creepy thing to do, then remembered his wife's demands regarding Christmas money to buy the kids presents. He was supposed to have been putting money aside for months but had been lying about it while betting on the horses. If the daft nags he picked would ever win, his wife would never know, and he could get her that bracelet she wanted. As it was, he needed every penny he could get.

'Sure thing,' he said. 'That will cost a little extra.'

In the back of the cab as it followed Matilda's lime green Fiat 500 around Clitheroe, Albert looked at the bottle of pills again.

Rex nudged Albert's arm and coaxed him to draw the right conclusion.

'The pills, old man. Come on, there's a good boy, you can make the connection. I took them from the dead man's mate. You've seen them before, remember?'

Albert read the bottle's label. He'd already noted that they were prescribed to Emelia Caan. Rex was taking a great interest in them though.

'You're trying to tell me something, aren't you?' he asked Rex.

Rex made a chuffing noise and wagged his tail.

'You think Mrs Caan might be involved in her husband's death?' he hazarded a wild guess.

More tail wagging, this time at twice the speed.

Albert squinted at the bottle. Even with his reading glasses on, the small type listing the active ingredient in the drug was too small for him to make out.

'You believe Mrs Caan poisoned her husband?'

Rex bounced up and onto his feet.

'Atta boy, old man. Well done. I'll make a detective of you yet.'

'He'll have to sit down,' warned the driver.

Rex lowered himself back to the seat but kept his head and eyes up to look at his human.

Albert was puffing out his cheeks and frowning.

'I don't see how that is possible, Rex.'

Rex's tail stopped wagging.

'The pills are intended for human consumption. I mean, sure, maybe she was crushing them up and stirring them into his coffee, but what would that do?' The only other part of the label he could read explained the drug had been prescribed to treat hypertension.

If she gave him a lot, would it mess with his heart? That was moot because he had been poisoned.

'It looks like the car is pulling up,' called the driver over his shoulder as he flicked his indicator on.

Albert glanced up and through the windscreen. The driver was about to pull into the same turning Matilda was taking.

'No! Keep going, please.' He shoved an arm through the gap between the front seats, urgently pointing along the road so the driver would keep going and not tip their hand. 'Pull up over there, please.'

Albert knew where Matilda was going. He didn't know why. Not yet at least. But he had a good idea.

Confused, but not exactly bothered – the old man was paying so he could be as nuts as he wanted – the cab driver cruised up to the kerb. They were parked in front of Parsons' Perfect Hotpots on the opposite side of the road.

The restaurant was locked up, the door displaying a sign that told everyone it was closed. It was as Albert expected since the proprietor was in hospital. So far as he knew, they were still closed anyway after the poisoning yesterday, but he did not know the outcome of the Food Health agents' visit.

Albert slid some notes from his wallet, thrusting them toward the driver without even looking to see how much he had in his hand.

'Come on, Rex,' he shoved the door open, checked for traffic, and dashed across the road.

The taxi driver flared his eyes at the fresh-from-the-mint notes in his hand; there was a great outsider running in the three o'clock at Ascot. He could clean up if it came in.

While behind them the cab pulled away, Albert and Rex rushed across the road to peer cautiously into the restaurant. Albert spotted movement in the kitchen at the back of the restaurant; a shadow moving through a shaft of light.

He ducked out of the way, hurrying along the street past the parade of shops to the same entrance Matilda drove into. It led, he knew already, to the goods yards behind the shops. The staff working in the businesses would park there and deliveries could be made without blocking the road.

It was also good for dark deeds as he remembered from the previous evening.

Rex couldn't work out what they were doing back at the hotpot place. His human seemed to understand that the dead man's mate was behind the murder, but then veered off course, arguing that the pills Rex found couldn't have done it.

He didn't know about that. He ate a hotpot last night … okay he ate two, but the point is they almost killed him. Perhaps killed might be too strong a term to employ, but Rex knew what he meant. The woman had drugs, she lied about being at the hotpot place, ergo she was the killer.

Albert led Rex toward the back entrance of Parsons' restaurant, the belt from a hospital robe doing its job only because Rex was willingly going with his human.

As they turned into the building's rear yard, an open area some five yards across and maybe eight yards deep, Albert paused beside a blood stain. The dark, almost black mark was where Danny had lain a few hours ago. It would need a hose and a hard broom to remove it.

What had he been doing here so late when his business had been forcibly shut hours earlier? Staying late to deal with paperwork might provide an easy explanation, but not when the man was as ill as Albert knew he was. Danny Parsons had been barely able to stand when Albert bluffed his way in as a Food Health agent.

Next to the stain was an industrial rolltop trash receptacle. Lifting the lid, Albert peered inside, saw what he expected to see, and closed it again.

At the back door, he sucked in a deep breath and questioned whether this was the right thing to do. He had a wild theory about Chris Caan's death and about who killed him. In the last day, he'd ruined what little credibility Dobbs had left, probably cost the man his job and dropped Selina in it. He still needed to call her to apologise and see what he could do to make amends.

Gripping the door handle, he decided he was right when he told Dobbs the only solution now was to see the whole thing through. If he didn't then not only might there be a terrible miscarriage of justice, but it would mean all that had befallen Dobbs and Selina was for naught.

He tapped Rex gently on the skull to get his attention and put a finger to his lips.

'We need to do this quietly, Rex, understand?'

Rex didn't know to nod, so he wagged his tail, just once, and stared at the door, waiting for it to open.

Albert turned the handle and pulled.

It swung outward to reveal Matilda carrying a box of hotpots. Her eyes were wide, and her mouth was hanging open as if caught in a silent scream.

Albert blocked the door and refused to move.

'Are those the ones laced with laxatives?' he asked.

Matilda couldn't work out whether to run or scream or simply deny everything. The problem with the last part was that she didn't know anything.

In the end, with the old man's eyes boring into her, she mumbled, 'I don't know.'

Albert twirled an inverted finger in the air, telling her to turn around. He followed it with a shooing motion - she was to go back inside.

Albert jerked Rex's makeshift lead, sending him into the building, and closed the door once they were all inside.

'My guess is that your dad asked you to get to the restaurant and dispose of all the hotpots, is that right?' Albert tried to make his voice friendly when he accused her.

Matilda bowed her head and nodded. Her cheeks were flushed red, and Albert expected to find she was on the verge of crying when she looked back up. He spared her his gaze and began to move around the kitchen as he talked.

'Your father was doing it himself last night, probably returning here after dark when he figured no one would see him. Unfortunately, Jack Marley was waiting for him, and the task never got finished.'

Matilda said nothing.

'I think your father chose to lace some hotpots with laxative. He fed one to Chris Caan when he came back to the restaurant yesterday afternoon.' Albert was guessing that part, but it made sense. 'Why did he do that? Does your father have reason to hate Chris Caan?'

215

Matilda looked up, her eyes brimming with tears as Albert expected.

Rex was sniffing the air. Nothing had been cooked in the small family restaurant for over a day, but it was still filled with glorious odours. He knew eating the hotpots yesterday had made him ill but that was no reason not to try them again, right?

Keeping one wary eye on his dog, Albert waited for an answer.

Matilda rolled one shoulder in a sort of shrug. 'I'm not sure,' she murmured. 'What I mean is I don't think so. Dad was so excited that the restaurant was going to be on TV. He said it would bring a huge boon to our sales. Dad was getting some stills blown up to display on the walls.' She stopped talking, looking very much like she was thinking about something and questioning whether to mention it.

Albert continued to watch her, staying deliberately silent so she would feel a need to fill the void with her words. He also took a pace to his right and tapped Rex's snout. The dog was running his nose along a counter edge, snuffling in the scents coming from the box filled with the hotpots Matilda had been taking outside.

Rex frowned but moved away from the food when his human crooked a finger at him.

'Why did Chris Caan come back here yesterday after everyone left?' Albert threw another question at the young woman.

Matilda muttered, 'I asked him this morning at the hospital. I asked Mrs Caan too when she came to visit.'

Boom! A tiny explosion went off in Albert's head.

If Rex could have fist pumped the air he would have done.

Chewing his lips in anticipation, Albert framed his next question carefully.

'Emelia Caan came to the hospital to visit your father this morning?'

'Yes. It was right before you showed up.' Matilda's face was a picture of innocence; she wasn't hiding anything.

'What did they discuss?' Albert pressed to know more.

This time she shrugged. 'I don't know. Dad sent me to get her a coffee and when I got back, she was already gone. Gran was in the toilet, so she didn't even know Mrs Caan had been in.'

Albert sucked on his teeth, frustrated with how difficult the mystery was proving to be.

'I wondered if it was connected to her coming to the restaurant right before Mr Caan yesterday,' Matilda volunteered.

Albert froze, piercing the young woman with his eyes.

'Your father, Danny Parsons, had a meeting with Emelia Caan here yesterday afternoon right before her husband was poisoned?'

'Yes. It was about an hour before Mr Caan returned.' Matilda looked guilty all of a sudden. She had let the cat out of the bag and there was no way to put it back in.

Rex sniggered. 'I told you she lied about coming here.'

Albert probed for more information.

'Were they alone? What did they talk about?' Albert was onto something now. How was it that no one else knew Emelia Caan met with Danny Parsons? Was Rex right all along? Was Emelia behind the poisoning and used Danny to deliver it? Was the laxative some kind of elaborate red herring? What then was Jack Marley's part in it all?

Matilda stuttered, 'I don't think I should talk about it.' Her voice was quiet. Unlike her grandmother, she didn't like confrontation. She was alone in the restaurant with an old man she didn't know and felt quite uncomfortable.

Albert had been about to shout at her, hoping that might shock her into revealing all that she knew. Instead, he saw how afraid she appeared and sent Rex to comfort her.

All it took was a head gesture from Albert. Rex had a natural inclination to go to humans when they were visibly upset. In his head, having him close was all it took to make people happy again.

'It's okay, Matilda,' Albert soothed. 'At worst your dad had been a pawn in someone else's game. We need to find out why and then clear his name if we can. The truth always comes out in the end. Keeping secrets has already landed your father in hospital. I was here last night, imagine what might have happened if I hadn't come along when I did.'

Until that moment, Albert hadn't thought about it in those terms. He wasn't looking for recognition or praise, but the fact remained that had he not been there, Matilda's father would not have survived his wound.

Almost too quiet to hear, as she ruffled the fur on Rex's head, Matilda whispered, 'I don't know what they talked about. They went into dad's office and closed the door. I heard dad shouting though.'

'And Chris Caan turned up a short while afterwards, yes?'

Matilda nodded, never raising her eyes to see Albert's face.

'It was about an hour after his wife left,' she repeated her earlier claim. Her head snapped up suddenly, 'She said she had to get to an appointment at a spa,' Matilda blurted. 'I don't know if that's important, but it is the one thing I did hear her say when she was rushing to leave.'

Albert's breaths were coming as gasps of excitement. Emelia Caan had come to the restaurant and delivered the poison. Maybe Danny didn't even know, though he must have suspected something otherwise why try to hide the evidence? She came to the restaurant and then rushed away to create her alibi. Did Emelia have something over Danny that she used to make him help her? Or was he keeping quiet because they were involved, and they both wanted rid of her husband?

Options and possibilities flitted around Albert's head.

He pushed her to reveal more. 'Matilda, I need you to think now. Did your father have any contact with Emelia Caan before yesterday? Did he ever mention her? Do they know each other or have any kind of history?'

Matilda didn't know. Albert believed her, but he did press her to open her father's computer and look at his social media profile. She was reluctant but bought into the idea that her dad might be mixed up in something that was going to get him into even more trouble if she didn't help the old man put a stop to it.

They went through his friends and his online messages but found no communication with, or trace of, either of the Caan's. In his emails was a folder containing all the communication about the TV show and what the film crew needed him to do. Mostly it was lists of what not to wear, and that professional makeup would be provided on the day, so Danny didn't need to worry about his hair and such. Otherwise, it was details about meetings in the lead up to filming.

Albert accepted there was nothing more to be learned at the restaurant. He had somewhere else to go and more questions to ask, but the net was closing, and he was the one holding both ends. He could feel the case narrowing into a funnel. Soon there would be no questions left to ask and he would hold all the pieces.

Just as he turned away from the screen, his eyes caught sight of a single line. It was the name at the bottom of the email.

'Shaun Romsey,' he read the name and said it aloud.

Matilda, sitting in front of the computer at Albert's request because he had no knowledge or tolerance for the infernal things, glanced up in question.

Albert pointed to the screen.

'It might be nothing more than coincidence, but I need to check. Can I ask you to look up that name?'

'Look it up,' Matilda questioned.

Albert wasn't sure what the right words were.

'Yes, Googlise it or internet search him. Use the social media thing to see if he is on there.'

'Oh, right,' Matilda managed to figure out what the old man was asking her to do. Three seconds later she had a picture of Shaun Romsey on the screen and a whole social media profile that told the world where he went to school, what he did for a living, plus his relationship status et cetera ad infinitum.

Albert wanted to see the man's photographs. The older the better, he expressed. Albert didn't have a social media profile; it wasn't something that interested him. But he had seen a few and possessed a basic understanding of how they worked and what information they possessed.

Checking to see if the name linked to an otherwise unremarkable clue provided him with yet another answer. It was a piece of the puzzle he hadn't even known existed but seeing the photographs and borrowing the mouse from Matilda and hovering over the faces so it revealed the names, he found out something that changed the entire case.

'Does this mean something?' Matilda asked when Albert failed to say anything for more than a minute.

Albert was leaning on the desk and staring down into the grain of the fake wood veneer. This case wasn't what he thought at all. A crazy theory was emerging from the dark recesses of his head. A faint memory of a case many, many years before held a clue to what might have happened. However, if he was even half right, proving it was going to take some doing.

His first thought was to call Selina. She would be able to get him the answer, but he knew he couldn't bother her again. He needed to call her to apologise, that was what he needed to do.

Matilda rapped her knuckles on the desk.

'Hello? Mr Smith? What is going on? Who is Shaun Romsey? Does he have something to do with what happened to Chris Caan?'

Albert shook his head. 'Shaun Romsey is just a name. He has nothing to do with anything.' With his cryptic remark delivered and his brain swirling madly, Albert clicked his fingers at Rex and started toward the door.

Matilda, confused and getting annoyed, leapt to her feet.

'Hey! What's happening. Where are we going now?'

Albert was halfway out the office door.

'We?'

School Days

Matilda refused to let the old man out of her sight. She believed her dad was an innocent pawn, just like Albert suggested he might be. Albert knew nothing of the sort, but he was convinced that Danny's attempts to give Chris Caan a bad case of trouser trouble with a heavy dose of laxatives had a reason behind it that was nothing to do with ending the man's life.

They were going to visit Danny's old school and since he now had Matilda in tow, whether he wanted her or not, he at least had a ride to get there.

Before he got in the car, he placed a call to Selina. Phoning her in the car on the way to the school was more efficient but he didn't want Matilda, or anyone else, to hear him begging his daughter for forgiveness.

Selina didn't answer her phone though. Albert tried a second time with the same result. Was she so miffed at him she was now refusing to pick up? That didn't sound like something she would do; Selina was too mature for that.

Huffing out a breath of disappointment, he accepted it for what it was. Matilda was waiting at her car.

The tiny Fiat didn't have back doors, so Rex had to clamber in through the front. Matilda folded her seat forward and then back again after the large dog bounded onto her back seat.

He completely filled the rear-view when she tried to reverse out and turn around, but he settled onto the seat and stretched out when Albert encouraged him to.

The school was across town, but the early afternoon traffic was light and the route she picked avoided most of the traffic lights that might have slowed them down.

'Gran still lives in the same house where dad grew up,' Matilda explained as she neared their destination. 'It's right by the school.'

She was just making conversation but planned to park her car at her gran's house and walk the rest of the way. Albert convinced her to park at the school right outside of the reception.

Sitting in a small office with a sign above bearing the legend 'Reception' a tiny woman with silver hair peered over the top of her bifocals as they approached.

'Matilda Parsons. Are you back to try again?' she asked in a loud voice.

'That's Miss Gertrude,' Matilda hissed from the corner of her mouth. 'She's worked here for about a hundred years and knows everyone in Clitheroe because most of them passed through this school at some point in the past. We all called her Miss Get Rude because she is so horrible. She never has anything nice to say to anyone.'

To Albert that just sounded like a challenge.

'Good afternoon,' he hallooed brightly, giving the sour-faced old bat the benefit of the doubt.

'It was,' she sneered. 'No dogs. You can take that filthy mongrel outside right now.'

'I think not,' Albert chuckled. 'Now, I need to speak to you about Danny Parsons and Jack Marley. Matilda tells me you know everyone. I have a mystery to solve and the need to pick your brains.'

He was being conspiratorial, but it didn't get him anywhere.

'I said out. Now,' she insisted, getting to her feet. 'Or I'll call the police and have you ejected.' She said it with a cruel smile, clearly hoping she would get to do so.

'No need,' said a voice from behind Albert and Matilda. 'The police are already here.'

As Miss Gertrude's face fell, Albert and Matilda turned to see who was there.

Rex already knew. He smelled him coming and had been facing out of the reception office and back across the lobby, wagging his tail as the familiar figure approached.

Constable Dobbs was back in uniform and unlike every other time Albert had seen him in it, it was smart, clean, and freshly ironed.

Albert stuck out his hand. 'Dobbs. Good to see you. What are you doing here?'

'I need that dog taken outside,' insisted Miss Gertrude again.

No one paid her any attention.

Dobbs sniffed and shrugged.

'Going out in a blaze of glory, I suppose. I figure they will take this uniform off me before the week is out. I might as well get some use out of it while I can.'

'Excuse me!' raged Miss Gertrude, not used to being ignored. Like many petty functionaries, she saw the school as her domain. She had been here through no fewer than twelve headmasters or headmistresses. The lazy little cow, Matilda Parsons, was right about one thing – she knew

225

everyone. She also knew almost everything about everyone and that made her powerful.

Dobbs loomed over the top of Albert and Matilda, sticking his head under the doorframe to look down at the tiny receptionist.

'Remember me?' he asked rhetorically.

Miss Gertrude smirked. 'Susie Dobbs, the big boy with the little girl's name. What a disappointment you turned out to be.'

He didn't need any time to think about his reply.

'Oh, shut up, you old cow.' Dobbs didn't spare her another look as he backed out of the doorway. 'Come on, there is someone much better to talk to than her.'

Yelling from her office, Miss Gertrude continued to issue threats. 'I'm calling the police!'

Over his shoulder, Dobbs repeated, 'I'm already here!' Turning a corner and getting out of sight, Dobbs led them to a set of stairs which he started to climb. 'I guess you know now why I go by my last name.'

Albert had wondered if Dobbs might tackle the subject himself.

It was Matilda who asked the question though. 'Did your parents really name you Susie?'

Dobbs nodded with a sigh. 'Dad split the second he found out mum was pregnant. I've never met him. Mum really wanted a little girl and the way she tells it, her mum and her gran and everyone else told her she was having a little girl – some nonsense about the shape of the belly. Anyway, by the time I arrived, she had a wardrobe full of girls' clothes, a pink pushchair … you get the picture, I'm sure. Mum went around telling everyone I was a girl and dressing me in girl clothes right up until I was about four. By then, she wasn't fooling anyone. I looked about as feminine as a naked, bearded lumberjack wearing lipstick as a disguise.'

The image painted a convincing picture.

Albert had to wonder what being called Susie might do to a chap's self-esteem. Nothing positive he felt sure.

At the top of the stairs, Dobbs turned right.

'Where are we going?' asked Matilda.

Albert was happily being led. He had no idea where Dobbs was taking them either but figured their destination would be revealed in time.

Rather than answer, Dobbs said, 'I got into lots of fights when I was here. As soon as the older boys in the classes above me found out about my name, the bullying started. No one on the staff seemed to care all that much, but there was one teacher who took me to one side. He gave me a job at breaktimes and lunchtimes and … well, it kept me out of the way and I'm not sure I would have made it through school in one piece if he hadn't.'

They arrived at a door marked 'Library'. Dobbs pushed it open and stood to one side so Matilda, Albert, and Rex could enter.

'Hello,' said a kindly voice that did not appear to have a body. 'Who do we have here?'

Stepping out from behind a bookcase, a small man wearing a rainbow pin on the left lapel of his bright orange jacket, greeted his visitors with a smile. That he was gay was not in question, and it answered a question about his need to protect Dobbs. The man was in his seventies which meant he had to live with his sexuality in a less evolved era.

227

Albert remembered how there were men he knew in the police who were shunned because there were rumours about them. Indeed, he was a serving police officer when homosexuality was decriminalised in 1967. It had never been a crime he had to pursue, but there were police officers dedicated to catching what at the time were considered deviants.

He reached out to shake the man's hand.

'Albert Smith.'

'Edgar Nancy,' the librarian replied. If there had been any remaining question as to why he thought it his task to rescue the young Dobbs from his playground tormentors, the man's last name answered them. Albert could only imagine how Edgar might have suffered in his youth.

Edgar turned his attention to his other guests.

'Matilda Parsons, isn't it?' he questioned before tracking his eyes more than a foot higher into the air. 'And Constable Dobbs. Good to see you again. To what do I owe the pleasure? I assume this is not a social visit.'

Dobbs got straight down to business, thanking Edgar for receiving them and offering to make the tea.

Matilda volunteered for the task, keen to have something useful to do.

'It's about Danny Parsons, that's Matilda's dad,' Dobbs explained unnecessarily. 'And Jack Marley. I remember you as one of life's great observers, Edgar. I'm hoping you can shed some light on any interaction they might have had with Chris Caan.'

'Oh, yes,' Edgar nodded sagely. 'Yes, I heard about poor Mr Caan. Poison, wasn't it?' Then he added up the dots and saw why Matilda was with them. He pursed his lips and thought for a moment.

Matilda brought him a steaming mug of tea and another for Albert before returning to the small table in the corner where Edgar had a kettle set up.

'Any biscuits?' asked Rex.

Albert stroked the dog's head and waited for the librarian to begin talking.

'If memory serves,' Edgar sipped at his tea before using a hand to clear a space on his desk for it, 'Chris Caan didn't go to this school.' He got to his feet again, weaving between Dobbs and Albert who had to shuffle their knees around to let him pass.

Rex peered around hopefully. 'Really? No biscuits?'

Across the room, Edgar ran a finger along a shelf, stopping it when he reached the volume he wanted. The shelf was filled with thick books that looked like encyclopaedias. Bound in black, Albert saw what they were only when Edgar lifted a tome from the shelf and carried it to the table.

'Each class gets their own album,' he explained, carefully donning a pair of white cotton gloves. 'It tracks their progress through the school and sometimes beyond if there are pages left and a student goes on to achieve something remarkable. There have been no fewer than three members of parliament who passed through this school, two Olympic athletes, one chart-topping popstar, and one convicted murderer. We don't dwell on the last one,' he added as he turned the first page.

Inside the album, the class register listed all the children. Albert and Dobbs got to their feet, cramming in either side of the librarian to get a better look.

'I can smell them, you know.' Rex made a show of snorting air into his nose audibly. 'It's no good pretending there are no biscuits here.' Bored with being ignored, he set off to find them for himself.

As the humans worked through the album of pictures and newspaper clippings, Rex snuffled his way around the room.

It took him less than twenty seconds to identify the drawer the biscuits were in. The humans were paying him no attention, which was both good and bad. If he could open the drawer, chances were he could devour what he found without them even noticing. However, the drawer had a recess to grip, not a handle to pull and that was enough to defeat him.

Back at Edgar's desk, the humans were indeed oblivious to the dog's plight. They were too engrossed in the mystery. Unfortunately, the scrap book wasn't shining any light on it. Danny and Jack appeared in several pictures and Edgar remembered that the two boys were friends. However, there was nothing to tie the boys to what was happening now.

Albert screwed up his face as he fought with the conflicting facts in his head.

'Wait a second. Matilda, your grandmother said your father knew Chris Caan. She made it sound like there was something that happened when they were kids, or maybe when they left school and were young men. There is something that links them.'

Matilda shrugged an apology. 'I can call him and ask,' she suggested. Albert shook his head. He wanted to say that would be cheating. This was a mystery so being told the answers defeated the object of investigating it. Suspecting that would just make him sound weird, he said something else.

'Your father has been trying to hide the truth from everyone. He is, I hate to say, lying to the police, so I doubt he will change his mind now. I believe we have to work this out for ourselves.'

Dobbs stood back from the desk, cupping his chin. Albert could see the constable was deep in thought and looked ready to say something profound.

'You have a question or a suggestion,' he prompted.

Dobbs twitched his eyes and dropped the hand holding his chin.

'Um, actually, I was wondering if there were any biscuits to go with the tea?'

Rex's front paws did a little happy dance next to the drawer which he then nudged with his nose.

Edgar snorted a laugh. 'It looks like the dog already found them.'

Rex rolled his eyes. Or he would have if that were a dog thing to do.

'What did you expect?' he asked. 'If you want to hide biscuits from a dog, you need to put them next to some strong peppermints. Anyway, let's get this drawer open and get to the part where we share the food.'

The biscuits were digestives, but not the chocolate covered kind, so Albert let Rex have one.

Muttering under his breath that one biscuit was hardly worth bothering with, Rex laid back down on the rug.

'Who's this?' asked Matilda.

While the men's attention was on the sweet treats, she had continued to turn the pages of the album. It was now open on a page toward the back where the students were now in their teens. It was their graduation year and a posed photograph with the children in three lines one behind the other.

Albert, Dobbs, and Edgar crowded around her, pressing in on all sides. Matilda's right index finger pointed to a pretty young girl. She was standing next to Jack Marley who had been awkwardly positioned in the back row despite being a foot shorter than most of the other boys. Even the girl to his left was a head taller. That wasn't what drew the eye though.

Unnoticed by the cameraman, and the teachers, no doubt, Jack Marley and the girl were holding hands. One could see their intertwined digits between the bodies of the middle row. Not only that, unless they were all very mistaken, the girl was the teenage version of Emelia Caan.

Albert sucked in a deep breath as a fat piece of the puzzle dropped into place.

'Does it say who she is?' he asked, squinting at the page where the names were listed below the photograph.

Matilda read it, 'Emelia Prentice.'

'Her maiden name,' Albert murmured. 'That's the connection. She was with Jack, but she ended up marrying Chris. I'm willing to bet she met Chris through Jack when they were at catering college together.' He tipped back his head and stared to heaven.

The how and why of what happened between the three was insignificant. They were linked and it went back years.

'Jack must have reached out to an old friend to help him with his business, but rather than come to Jack Marley's aid, Chris Caan chose to destroy him. Jack wanted revenge against them both.'

'But you said he didn't kill Chris Caan,' Dobbs pointed out. 'You were most insistent about it.'

Albert nodded. 'That's because he didn't. He wanted to though. I think he even intended to. That's where Danny Parsons comes in.'

Dobbs wasn't able to keep up. 'So Danny killed Chris?'

'He most certainly did not,' snapped Matilda.

Albert sucked on his bottom lip for a second. 'No, he didn't.'

Matilda slapped Dobbs on the arm.

'See.'

Albert pulled a face. 'Except, I think he sort of did.'

He got three sets of raised eyebrows in response. The only one in the room who did not question his latest cryptic statement was Rex.

Rex had noticed the biscuits were unguarded on the side by the kettle. All he had to do was nimbly extract one without rustling the packet.

Edgar felt a need to press Albert for clarity.

'I'm sorry. You said that Danny Parsons didn't kill Chris Caan, but actually he did. I'm not following.'

'Nor am I,' agreed Dobbs who accepted that he usually had no idea what was going on.

'No. Me either,' added Matilda who was not happy her father was being implicated in a murder. 'I thought we were clearing his name, not framing him.'

Her cross expression was warranted but Albert wasn't ready to show everyone his hand yet. He downed the remainder of his tea and placed the mug on the desk with a determined thump.

'We need to go. Dobbs, I think we can save your job or, at least, make it difficult for them to sack you. Matilda, I think your father is hip-deep in this but, if I am right, he might come out of it okay.' He twisted on his heels to look across the room. 'Rex!'

Rex jumped. 'What? I'm not doing anything.' Digestive biscuit crumbs rained down from his lips.

'Come on, dog. We've a case to sew up.'

Rex took a last longing look at the packet of digestives sitting tantalisingly close to the edge of the counter. If he chose to be a bad dog, he could snaffle a few more of them before his human could even cross the room.

With a sigh, he let them go.

'Is this where you finally admit I was right and have the dead man's mate arrested?' Rex got no answer to his question and didn't really expect one. He didn't employ his nose to search out clues for his own glory, of course. He wasn't after recognition. A bone to chew might be nice though.

Edgar grabbed his coat as his guests began filing to the door.

'I'm coming too. This is far too intriguing to miss.'

Making their way back down the stairs toward reception, Dobbs caught sight of squad cars in the school carpark.

'Uh-oh.' He pointed. 'We might need to take a back door out of here.'

Albert spotted Detective Inspector Brownlow's vintage Jaguar.

'I think you might be right,' he agreed.

Confused, Edgar asked, 'Are you not all on the same side?'

Albert wished they were. 'Not exactly,' he admitted. 'Dobbs the time for action is upon us. We need to assemble several people all in one place.'

'Right. Yes. Of course.' Dobbs made sure to sound like that was his plan too. However, after a few seconds, he had to ask, 'Who?'

Expert Testimony

Albert outlined his plan, rough as it was, and sent Dobbs on his way. Matilda went with him to give a hand since she knew some of the people involved.

Edgar stayed with Albert who had a special request for the librarian.

'A chemistry teacher?' Edgar questioned.

'Yes. Might need the school nurse and a biology teacher too,' he scratched his chin. 'Actually, maybe the whole science department might be best.'

Edgar had no idea what Albert wanted them for but led him through the school asking questions as they went.

Albert remained tight-lipped but did explain the need for expert opinion. The school bell rang while they were wending their way along a corridor.

'Watch out!' called Edgar, pinning himself to a wall and urging Albert to do the same with Rex.

A nanosecond later, as if the classrooms were pressurised, children of all ages, shapes and sizes burst from doors in front and behind. They were loud and unruly and excited. It was the end of the school day, and they were going home.

Rex was used to crowds and noise; his training as a police dog took care of that, but even so the confined space and so many small people made him nervous.

Albert kept him close, tucking his tail out of the way so it would not get trodden on and the three of them became a rock at the edge of a stream.

The children flowed past and around them. Some even choosing to spin like eddies in the giddiness of their excitement.

A minute later, they were alone in the corridor once more.

'We'll have to be quick,' warned Edgar, setting off at a brisk pace. 'The teachers won't hang around for long either.'

They were quick enough to catch them, and Edgar's unexpected appearance plus Albert's tale proved sufficient to capture their interest. Chemistry, biology, and even physics teachers leaned in to hear his questions and hypothesise answers. They would need to conduct experiments, but with half a dozen of them jumping online to conduct on the spot research, they quickly concluded Albert could be right.

It was hardly a fist pump moment. If anything, it made Albert feel sad to have his crazy theory confirmed.

'What now?' asked Edgar. 'Who were those people you asked young Dobbs to collect?'

Solemnly Albert huffed out a sigh and said, 'They are Chris Caan's killers.'

Edgar reacted as if jabbed with a sharp stick. 'What, all of them?'

Albert sucked his cheek. 'Yes and no.'

Edgar couldn't stop his eyebrows from frowning and then rising and then frowning again. The old man sounded lucid enough, but he wasn't making any sense. He'd barraged the school's science department with questions about odd chemical compounds but hadn't sufficiently explained why it was important.

He could tell Edgar was winding up to ask another question, so he cut him off by asking one of his own.

'Can anyone spare me an hour to give expert testimony and solve a murder?'

Carpark Standoff

With Edgar and three science teachers – who thought this was a jolly jape to get involved in – on his heels, Albert made his way back through the school. He didn't want to sneak out a side door to avoid reception and the possibility that he would run into DI Brownlow again, but he also accepted she would, at the very minimum, delay his rendezvous with Dobbs, Matilda, and their host of guests.

Unfortunately, DI Brownlow proved to be too wily for Albert to evade and she caught him the moment he reached the carpark.

'Stop!' she commanded, jabbing her arm at two uniformed constables, and sending them to intercept.

Standing next to the detective inspector was Miss Gertrude. The tiny woman had a satisfied grin on her face and no doubt something unpleasant and gloating to say.

Albert did as instructed, planting his feet and waiting for the constables to arrive.

'Is there a problem, Detective Inspector?' he called loud enough for her to hear.

The teachers from the science department were looking at each other and at the approaching police officers in confusion. What had been a bit of fun a moment ago was now decidedly less so. Was the old man not the good guy?

'Ha!' heckled Miss Gertrude. 'You're in for it now!'

DI Brownlow ignored the unpleasant receptionist, instructing her to stay where she was – not that Miss Gertrude did – as she moved to join her constables.

'Mr Smith you are becoming a problem for me. Why do I find myself at a school investigating a disturbance?'

Albert was pleased with the question.

'Yes, why indeed?' he let his reply hang in the air for a few seconds, letting it sink in. 'Perhaps you would like to explain why a detective inspector feels a personal need to respond to a minor, non-violent, non-crime related report? On a slow day, this might require a single constable to pop in just for public relations purposes.'

DI Brownlow had to fight her rising ire. The old man was one hundred percent on the money and her boss would see it that way too.

'You've no right to be here!' snarled Miss Gertrude rudely.

'Miss Gertrude, please,' begged Brownlow. Choosing to ignore Albert's question because it was inconvenient, she delivered the point she felt was most pertinent.

'Mr Smith you have been interfering with my investigation since you arrived in Clitheroe yesterday afternoon. In just twenty-four hours, you have tampered with evidence, badgered witnesses, potentially perverted the cause of justice, and led that idiot Dobbs into sabotaging his own career. I should thank you for the last one, I suppose.'

Albert kept his lips together and waited for her to finish.

'If Jack Marley slips through the net and is able to escape a conviction for killing Chris Caan, it will be due to your interference. I can tolerate no further meddling on your part, so to that end I am placing you under arrest for the crime of ...'

'Belay that order!'

The shout came from the carpark where a broad-shouldered man in chief constable's uniform was heading their way. He wasn't alone. To his right was another man of roughly the same age. He held himself in much the same way and though he was wearing a suit, Albert was willing to bet he was another high-ranking police officer.

Largely his assessment and guess were based on the third person with them. Just ahead of the two men was a woman. In her fifties, tall and athletic with long brunette hair shot through with grey and pulled into a tight ponytail, she was striding over the tarmac with purpose. It was her voice that interrupted DI Brownlow's arrest.

Albert was surprised to see her; he had no idea why she was here, but it explained why she hadn't answered her phone.

'Hello, Selina,' he gave her a wave.

Rex recognised the female human approaching as one of his human's pups. He wagged his tail in an appropriate manner.

Some of the colour drained from DI Brownlow's face.

'Selina?' she questioned, her eyes swinging from the approaching woman to the old man and back again. 'Selina Oxmore?'

Selina narrowed her eyes slightly.

'Chief Inspector Oxmore, if you please. Since you seem intent on making trouble for me, don't expect any professional courtesy in return.'

The two constables surrounding Albert and the party of school staff exchanged nervous glances.

DI Brownlow swung her head around to address the men arriving behind Selina.

'What is this, boss?'

Albert filled in the blanks. The man in uniform was DI Brownlow's chief constable. When she reported Selina for discussing the investigation with her father – a civilian – it reached the ears of Selina's boss who then called Brownlow's boss and here they all were trying to straighten things out in the spirit of mutual cooperation.

Brownlow's chief inspector introduced his equal.

'DI Brownlow this is Chief Constable Rivers. I think we all need to head back to the station for a little chat about protocol.'

Incensed, DI Brownlow pointed out, 'Sir, she is the one who broke protocol.'

'She is still your superior,' growled Selina. 'You will keep a respectful tongue in your head.'

Edgar nodded to his colleagues. 'Um, perhaps we ought to leave you all to it.'

Albert was swift to react, touching Edgar's sleeve as he begged, 'Please do not go anywhere.' Turning his attention to the gaggle of police officers, he said, 'I have no wish to cause any bother, yet I realise in doing what I do best, I have unintentionally achieved exactly that.'

'Yes, you have,' agreed DI Brownlow unnecessarily. She was rewarded with a frown from her chief constable.

Albert pressed on.

'The information my daughter, Chief Inspector Oxmore, passed me was not sensitive and has not been shared with a third party.'

'That is what I have explained already,' Selina pointed out.

Albert gave her a nod and ploughed on.

'However, while you will no doubt wish to investigate the subject of protocols and secrecy, there is a more pressing matter to which I hope you will allow me to attend. I suspect, in fact, that you may wish to accompany me.'

'You solved it, didn't you?' chuckled Selina, unsurprised to hear her father was calmly declaring that he alone knew the answer to the riddle of Chris Caan's death.

The Big Reveal

When they filed into Danny Parsons' hospital room, they joined Constable Dobbs who was shocked to find his chief constable coming through the door. He snapped out a smart salute or, at least, he tried to. Swinging upward, his right hand smacked into the monitor set next to Danny's bed, whacking it a yard across the room to crash into the wall.

Dobbs swore and sucked his fingers.

Matilda was back holding her father's hand and Pauline, though her eyes were still narrowed in Albert's direction, kept quiet when he entered the room.

Danny's family were not the only ones in the room though. Jasper and Rachel Grainger were there too. They were not together, Albert noted, standing about as far apart in the confined space as they could get. Emelia Caan was also in the small room, sitting on a chair by the window and looking very impatient.

Albert gave Dobbs a nod.

'Well done, Constable Dobbs. Any trouble?'

'Getting them to come? Not really.'

'What are we doing here?' Emelia demanded to know. 'And who are all these people?' she referred of course to the two chief constables, Selina, Edgar, and the science teachers who were now all crammed into the private hospital room.

It was a tight enough space before, but now it was close to standing room only.

Rex, permitted into the hospital because the town's police chief constable insisted it was necessary, narrowed his eyes at Emelia Caan and growled softly.

She hadn't noticed the dog until that point and could only see the tips of his ears over the bed when she looked to see what the noise was.

'Waaaah!' she leapt to her feet, startling everyone in the room. 'Waaah! It's that mad dog again! Get him away from me! He tried to kill me earlier!'

Everyone in the room swung their eyes to stare at Rex.

He yawned and looked about, showing his disinterest by lying down with his head on his front paws.

'Yes,' agreed Albert. 'Absolutely ferocious.'

His comment got a few sniggers.

While Emelia settled back into her chair, eyeing Rex warily, Albert gathered his thoughts. He was getting ready to lay them out. He still hadn't figured out what happened with Emelia and Jack all those years ago, and he wasn't sure quite what part Danny had played and that meant the next few minutes were going to be tricky.

He knew how Chris Caan was killed and who was to blame, but now he needed to trick them into revealing the parts he didn't know.

With all eyes on him, Albert licked his lips and decided to start with Danny.

'Mr Parsons,' he stopped and restarted. 'Danny, you have known Jack Marley since you were children.' Albert held up his hand to stop the man from speaking. 'There's no need to confirm it. You came to know Emelia when she came to the school as a transferee. What year was that?' he aimed the question at Emelia who chose to look bored and not answer.

'We were in year ten,' Danny confirmed.

Albert nodded in thanks and continued talking.

'Emelia and Jack were dating for a time, were they not?' He stopped moving to lock eyes with the man in the hospital bed and waited for his answer.

Danny Parsons had been keeping quiet since Chris Caan dropped dead on his premises and had no intention of changing that policy now. Jack couldn't say anything without making things worse for himself. At least that's what Danny thought until Albert spoke again.

'Jack is keeping quiet for now, but that won't last. He knows he didn't kill Chris Caan, Danny,' he lowered his voice so it came out almost as a comforting hug, a piece of friendly advice. 'He intended to though, didn't he? You knew he was planning something. Was it going to happen at the live event scheduled to take place in the town square last night?'

The flash of panic crossing Danny Parsons' eyes was all the confirmation Albert needed.

'You knew Jack was going to do something and he wasn't listening to reason. He was your oldest friend – you couldn't let him go through with it. And you couldn't go to the police either. That would be a terrible thing to do when Jack was already such a broken man.'

'Chris destroyed him,' Danny blurted.

Albert nodded his understanding.

'Jack thought Chris would help him, didn't he? That's why he contacted him. Jack believed his old flame Emelia,' Albert noticed how rigid Chris Caan's widow went at the mention of her name, 'and the man he lost her to would do him a favour from their lofty position.'

Danny shot a hard glare across the room at Emelia. 'They were just cruel. There was no need for Chris to write the things he did. He could have helped Jack.'

'You tried to warn Chris when he was at the restaurant yesterday morning, but he wouldn't listen. You knew Jack was going to do something rash and you did your best to prevent it from happening.'

Danny's breathing was starting to get heavy. How did the old man know all this? His pulse hammered in his chest, and he began to feel faint.

Albert's voice was building in volume and momentum.

'Jack was at the restaurant last night because he heard about Chris Caan's death and he knew it had to be you, didn't he, Danny? When Chris Caan refused to listen, you invited Emelia to come to the restaurant so you could talk sense into her. She didn't listen either, did she?' Albert's voice was getting louder and when he swung his head in Emelia Caan's direction, he did so with accusing eyes.

'She wouldn't listen and in a final ditch effort to prevent Jack from carrying out his murderous plan, you called Chris Caan and offered to give him your secret recipe. Isn't that what happened?' Albert was almost shouting now, battering the wounded man with his words. 'It has won you so many awards, did you promise to let him have it? You knew he was going to be attacked by Jack Marley and you had no way to stop it from happening, did you?'

'No,' winced Danny Parsons, tears brimming in his eyes. 'No one would listen.'

'You could have gone to the police,' Albert raged, 'but instead you chose to take matters into your own hands. You put laxatives into the hotpot didn't you, Danny? You fed Chris Caan poisoned food to save his life.'

'Yes,' Danny wailed, the truth tumbling from his lips as he started sobbing. His eyes were closed, and he was crushing Matilda's hand, he was gripping it so tight.

Albert let his voice return to a normal volume.

'How long did it take for Chris to start getting sick, Danny?'

Danny sobbed. 'Minutes. It was minutes. The laxative packet said it was fast-acting, but I figured it would still take an hour or more.' He opened his eyes and stared up at Matilda who had tears streaming down her cheeks. 'I killed him. I never meant to, but I killed him.'

'No, you didn't,' argued Albert.

Emelia Caan jumped to her feet.

'What are you talking about, you senile old fool. He just admitted it.'

Around the room, the expression on everyone's face made it clear they either agreed with Chris Caan's widow or were so hopelessly lost they now had no idea what was going on.

Albert ignored the jibe at his mental state and corrected her. 'What he admitted to was putting laxative into food which he then gave to your husband. The laxative, while unpleasant, is not deadly. Danny proved that himself when the police turned up.'

DI Brownlow felt she needed to say something. Her whole investigation had revolved around the fact that Danny Parson ate the hotpot and proved it wasn't that which had poisoned Chris Caan. Had she not been so busy today trying to make sure the amateur sleuth didn't mess up her investigation, she would have got to read the toxicology report she knew to be sitting on her desk.

'What point are you trying to make, Mr Smith? This is all very interesting, and yes, you have uncovered some facts that might seem pertinent to the case, but ultimately you have shown that Mr Parsons did not kill Chris Caan. That is precisely what I concluded more than twenty-four hours ago. What is it that you are attempting to prove?'

Albert held up his index finger.

'Ah, but the thing is, my dear detective inspector. Danny Parsons did kill Chris Caan.'

About ten different people exclaimed, 'What!'

Only Selina smiled. She'd endured a childhood of her father being cryptic and he had only gotten worse with age.

Matilda couldn't hold her tongue any longer.

'Mr Smith, you said you were going to clear all this mystery up. I'm more confused than ever before.'

He dipped his head, a small apology for the long route he was taking.

'Samuel Romsey,' he announced.

If possible, he got even more confused looks than before.

'Who's that?' asked Emelia.

Albert hadn't been looking at her. He was looking at Rachel. Her cheeks were suddenly bright red and she bore a look of intense horror. Albert judged that were there not so many people in the way, she might have bolted.

'Do you know how I know that name?' His eyes never left Rachel's. There was no doubt he expected her to answer. When she didn't, he said, 'It was on the bottle of Viagra pills you took from your father, Rachel.'

Jasper jolted. He'd been leaning on the wall, looking bored and wondering why his presence was required. Now he was taking a distinct interest.

DI Brownlow was equally involved.

'It's your father's?' she enquired, her question also aimed at Rachel who still wasn't talking. 'What was it doing in Chris Caan's roo …' her voice trailed off as the obvious answer presented itself.

'I knew it!' Jasper blew his top. 'All this time you've been denying it, but you really were sleeping with him, weren't you?' He started forward and found his way blocked by Constable Dobbs.

'That's enough now, sir. This is not the place.'

Albert watched Dobbs and watched his chief constable watching Dobbs. Whatever might have gone before, Dobbs was on display now and had acted and spoken exactly as he should.

Looking at DI Brownlow, Albert said, 'I assume you dismissed the bottle of Viagra?'

Frustrated, she admitted, 'I could find no connection between it and the case. Samuel Romsey appeared to be a red herring. I thought the bottle of pills had to be left behind by a previous occupant.'

Generously, Albert said, 'It was an easy mistake to make. I got lucky when I found the connection to Rachel Grainger.' Having named her, he then pierced the TV producer with a hard glare. 'Did he know you were slipping him the pills?'

Rachel's eyes went wide, and her face turned even redder than before. The shock and dread she felt was only visible for a second before her face crumbled and she covered it with her hands. Folding in on herself, she sagged against the wall as painful sobs racked her body.

'He was ...' she started but couldn't get the words out. 'He was ...'

'Performance issues, was it?' sneered Jasper.

Reacting to the sound of her husband's voice her head snapped back up, but she wasn't looking at him. Her face had become a mask of rage and when she spoke it was through gritted teeth.

'What difference does this make? Viagra isn't harmful.'

'Neither are laxatives,' pointed out Constable Dobbs in a helpful manner.

'I had nothing to do with Chris' death,' Rachel argued.

Albert sniffed in a deep breath to settle himself again.

'Oh, but you did, Rachel. You are as much to blame as Danny Parsons.'

'How?' demanded DI Brownlow. 'So far you have shown that two people were slipping the deceased two harmless drugs. What are you suggesting? That the two somehow combined to form a poison that killed him?'

Albert twisted his upper body, looking around for the science teachers. They were behind him by the door where they had been listening with rapt fascination.

Looking at them, he asked a question.

'What is the active ingredient in most laxatives?'

'Acarbose,' all three science teachers replied simultaneously as if trained to do so.

'And the same question about Viagra?' Albert coaxed.

This time just one of the teachers answered, the head of department.

'Sildenafil citrate.'

DI Brownlow's chief constable raised his hand to get Albert's attention as he started speaking.

'Are you really saying those two things combined to kill him?'

Albert gestured with his eyes for the science head of department to answer.

The man looked about, a little nervous to be put on the spot.

'Well, this isn't exactly my area of expertise, but the short answer is no.'

DI Brownlow threw her arms in the air.

'It would take a third ingredient to react with the Sildenafil. Basically, Sildenafil citrate is a perfectly safe drug to take, yet there are certain other chemicals it should not be mixed with.'

'Such as?' Albert prompted.

'Well, Levitra nitrates are one of the drugs commonly avoided. The two medicines work directly against one another and are likely to cause a massive drop in blood pressure.'

Albert reached slowly and deliberately into his pocket and withdrew the bottle of pills he had there. He threw it to Dobbs.

'Why don't you read the active ingredients for me,' he encouraged.

Dobbs squinted at the label, his lips moving as he tried to piece together some of the long names employed for the chemicals used. After two seconds, he gave up and just looked for the one he needed.

'It's right here,' he held the bottle up for all to see, not that anyone would be able to read it unless they had it in front of their face.

Holding the floor still, Albert's voice was sad when he revealed, 'One of the known side effects with hypertension drugs is erectile dysfunction.' He glanced at Rachel. 'That's why you felt the need to employ Viagra, my dear. Of course,' Albert swung his head and eyes round to meet Emelia's, 'it wasn't his hypertension but yours. You suspected his affair and were giving him your pills to make him floppy. His blood pressure was dangerously low, not that anyone knew it. No doubt the autopsy will show that to be the case. The two drugs you were each giving him in secret were having a desperately adverse effect on his body.' Albert looked across to Danny with an apologetic expression. 'When you then fed him Acarbose, it combined with the diuretics in Emelia's hypertension medication, his blood sugar level shot up and combined with his low blood pressure caused his entire body to shut down.'

Turning slowly on the spot, Albert met the eyes of the three people he was accusing and reached the only conclusion possible.

'A man lost his life and while each of you might have had your reasons for giving him the drugs you secretly administered, you are all to blame for his death.'

Emelia sneered, 'Can you prove any of that?'

Rex bounded under the hospital bed to pop up on the other side where he barked fiercely in her face.

She screamed, 'Arrrgh! Okay, okay, I admit it! I did it! I gave Chris my medication!'

Rex sat down again, pleased with his work.

Ultimately, Albert didn't have to prove anything. That was down to the Crown Prosecution Service. They would have a copy of the toxicology report which would establish the presence of the drugs in Chris Caan's body, and the autopsy would be able to prove exactly how he died. Albert had guessed a lot of it, most especially that part about how the drugs killed him, but they were educated guesses following the research the science teachers performed.

All the information was there on the internet to be found, some of it was stark warnings about the side effects of taking drugs your doctor had not prescribed.

Both Rachel and Emelia were taken into custody; they had questions to answer. Albert doubted either would go to jail – the Crown Prosecution Service stood to gain nothing by their incarceration. However, the investigation would continue until they were satisfied they had the right conclusion.

Danny admitted that Jack Marley had intended to kill Chris Caan and Emelia. It happened when he'd had far too much to drink one night.

Danny assumed it was nothing but hyperbole; a man spouting nonsense through his anger. It wasn't though, and Danny could not make his old friend see reason.

He then revealed that it was his fault he got stabbed. The knife was one of his own, on the tray of hotpots he was taking to the bin so he could use it to sweep them off the tray without his fingers touching them.

When Jack turned up, the knife was in Danny's right hand. Jack thought Danny meant him harm and they fought. Jack didn't take the weapon with him which meant the assault with a deadly weapon was not premeditated and thus his sentence would be less severe.

Of course, what Jack really needed was counselling and help for his mental health issues and he would get it, Albert felt sure, as part of his rehabilitation.

The case raised by DI Brownlow against Selina was dropped by her boss; he didn't need the paperwork and the breach of confidentiality was tenuous at best.

He couldn't prove it, and didn't have the energy to try, but Albert believed DI Brownlow had seen him as a threat to her record and continuing advancement. She was a good cop but found herself distracted when she found out who he was and the arrests he had recently been credited with. The bust in Dundee was especially present in her mind because the ink on the arrest reports there was barely even dry.

Leaving the hospital with Selina at his side and Rex trotting contentedly by his feet, Albert felt relaxed and happy.

Selina hooked an arm into the crook of his elbow. 'What would you like for dinner, Dad? My boss suggested we wait here until this evening before attempting to travel south; the roads will be terrible if we go now. We can have dinner together.'

Albert smiled to himself.

'Not hotpot.'

Epilogue: Change of Career

The following morning, Albert neatly folded his clothes - freshly laundered by the hotel - and packed away his meagre belongings. He and Rex had been on the road for weeks now and he had to admit he rather liked travelling.

He would have to go home eventually, he knew that, and had been waiting to start feeling homesick. If nothing else, he would run out of places to visit on his list of famous British foods. There was, however, another idea brewing at the back of his head, and he had to wonder if it might form the basis for a whole new adventure when this one came to an end.

Looking around the room to make sure he had everything, Albert spotted a piece of folded paper on the floor. He bent to pick it up and was about to throw it in the bin when he realised what it was.

Frowning slightly, he murmured, 'It must have dropped out of my wallet,' as he unfolded it to confirm what it was.

The betting slip from the turf accountant in Melton Mowbray had been in his wallet since he placed the bet and might have stayed there forever had it not fallen out. Studying the thin slip of paper, he was forced to acknowledge that he never had checked whether the horse he bet on had won or not.

Taking his reading glasses from an inside jacket pocket, he scrutinised the tiny letters printed across the two inch by four inch betting slip and wondered what 'season accumulator' meant.

It was a question for another day.

With the betting slip refolded and tucked safely back into a crevice in his wallet, Albert clicked his tongue to get Rex moving, picked up his small suitcase and backpack, and left the room. It was a short hop to Blackpool, hardly any distance at all and he would arrive in time for lunch or thereabouts.

In the lobby downstairs, he was pleased and surprised to find Dobbs waiting for him. Dobbs wasn't in uniform, though as Albert understood it, Dobbs was due to be off duty today just as he was supposed to be yesterday. Albert wanted to ask whether the chief constable had spoken to him already, but Dobbs got in first.

'I quit,' Dobbs admitted without preamble.

It came as a shock to Albert.

'Yeah, I knew I was a terrible cop. It just never really interested me, and I think the last couple of days showed me that.'

'So you just quit?' Albert wanted to clarify.

'Yup,' Dobbs smiled broadly and claimed proudly. 'I signed the paperwork with HR first thing this morning and came straight here to thank you.'

'Thank me?'

'I think I might have bumbled along in that job for years if it weren't for you showing me just how poorly suited I was.'

Albert blushed. 'That was not my intention.'

Dobbs chuckled. 'Probably not, but it's the best thing that ever happened to me. My uncle offered me a pub to run already. Under his guidance, of course, but when it came down to it, and I was asking myself what I did like to do, the answer is beer and football. I get to do both all the time if I am a publican.'

It was a twisted kind of logic, yet Albert could not fault it. Dobbs had been peculiarly bad as a police officer, but might make a fine pub landlord.

'I've got to go, actually,' Dobbs tapped his wristwatch. 'Uncle Pete is showing me around a brewery shortly.'

They shook hands and making Sue behind the hotel's reception counter wait for him, Albert watched the former Constable Dobbs jog across the lobby and out of the front door with more enthusiasm than he had seen from the man since they met.

Looking down at Rex, as Rex looked up at him, Albert smiled.

'You know what, boy?' I think it's going to be a great day.'

Rex only had one thing to say.

'I told you the dead man's mate did it.'

The End

Author's Note

Hello, reader,

Thank you for joining me at the back of the book. If this is somehow the first of my books you have ever read, then you have missed the previous fifty something notes which stand as a time marker for my life and for what is happening in the world around me.

It is summer here in England and Wimbledon is about to start. I mention the famous tennis tournament because it holds a special place in my heart. As a serving British soldier, I was able to perform a special duty there and got to spend four consecutive years enjoying the event in a privileged and intimate way. I got to explore the tunnels beneath the courts and go to the places normal people can never hope to access. Each year when the grass court season begins, I find myself unable to resist reminiscing about all the amazing matches I got to watch.

Why am I rambling on so much about the tennis? Because my writing time is about to go sideways, that's why. Since going full time as an author, I have barely taken any time off. Each day, I rise early and start pounding the keyboard. It is a pleasure, not a chore, but I might have to severely curtail my working hours for the next two weeks because Wimbledon is on, and it is what one does.

That and Pimm's. I shall watch the tennis and drink Pimm's. I would have been tempted to do the same last year but of course the tennis, like everything else, didn't happen.

That brings me nicely to Covid; the cause of last year's lack of sporting history. The current hopeful rumour is that the facemasks will be abandoned next month. It is the one thing I want to be free of, though to be fair, I hardly ever leave the house so rarely wear one. I have had both my injections, the rest of the population is getting theirs, and we appear, fingers crossed, to be coming to the end of the restrictions.

Long may it continue.

If you are not from England, you may have wondered what a Rich Tea biscuit is. A rather dry, an ultimately boring (in the author's opinion) biscuit, they are commonplace here. In the States, they would be called a cookie, but I am not sure you have anything like them. Designed, I believe, to hold their form when dunked into tea, they were originally produced in Yorkshire in the 17th century as a snack to eat between meals.

This book, the ninth in the series, was easier to write than many. I came into it with a strong idea about what the story was and how it would all end. I had to spend a few hours researching drugs and trying to figure out what would react with what to cause the effect I describe. Despite that claim to have done research for this book, it is fiction and the death as I describe it, should be considered the same.

There are those authors out there who painstakingly ensure their facts are factual. Ballistics must be spot on, the effect on the body of a particular drug recorded at a level that would stand up to medical scrutiny. I am not that author. My focus is on the story, and if that means I say a thing can happen, when actually it cannot, I apologise to anyone offended, but I am probably going to do it again.

Maybe I would be safer writing time travel stories. Though perhaps I would get even more people arguing and pointing out inaccuracies then.

I am stuck now with the difficult task of deciding what to write next. I have a plethora of options. Albert and Rex are off to Blackpool, and just like with this story, I have a clear picture of what is going to happen.

If you didn't notice it, there was a tiny reference to the likelihood of further Rex and Albert adventures. To be clear, when they return from this trip around the British Isles, which they will, the series will end. The current plan is for that to occur at book fifteen, but we shall see where my writing takes me. Then, a new series will start.

To keep things fresh, Albert will team up with another elderly gentleman for a trip around Europe. There is even a third series planned where Albert and Rex cross the pond to visit States. There, and accompanied by one of his children, they will tour the nation in a Winnebago and sample some of the famous dishes we all know. Or the US trip might be series two. I haven't decided yet.

I know where they are going, and what they will get up to. For you to find out, you will just have to keep reading.

Take care.

Steve Higgs

History of the Dish

Lancashire hotpot is a stew originating from Lancashire in the Northwest of England. It consists of lamb or mutton and onion, topped with sliced potatoes, and baked in a heavy pot on a low heat.

In Lancashire before industrialisation, families would work at home spinning thread while scrags of mutton stewed slowly over a low fire. Family members could attend to the cooking over many hours. In the initial stages of industrialisation and urbanisation, both men and women of all ages had long, strictly regulated work hours that made it impossible to cook food that required extensive attention and preparation time. Often lacking their own cooking facilities, housewives would carry a pudding or stew to the baker's oven and leave it there to cook.

It is often thought that the hotpot referred to is the dish in which the casserole is cooked. However, it is more likely to refer to the idea of a jumble or hodge podge of ingredients in the filling. Sir Kenelm Digby's 1677 *The Closet Opened* contains a recipe for the "Queen Mother's Hotchpot of Mutton". Similarly, *Mrs Beeton's Cookery Book* contains a recipe for "Hotch Potch", calling for neck of mutton, onion, carrot, peas, cauliflower, and lettuce.

Recipe

Ingredients

- 100g/3.5oz dripping or butter
- 900g/30oz stewing lamb, cut into large chunks
- 3 lamb kidneys, sliced, fat removed
- 2 medium onions, chopped
- 4 carrots, peeled and sliced
- 25g/1oz plain flour
- 2 tsp Worcestershire sauce
- 500ml/2 cups lamb or chicken stock
- 2 bay leaves
- 900g/30oz potato, peeled and sliced

Method

- **STEP 1**
  Heat oven to 160C/fan 140C/gas 3.
- **STEP 2**
  Heat a little of the 100g dripping or butter in a large
  shallow casserole dish and brown 900g stewing lamb chunks in
  batches, lift to a plate, then repeat with 3 trimmed and sliced
  lamb kidneys.
- **STEP 3**
  Fry 2 chopped onions and 4 peeled and sliced carrots in the pan
  with a little more dripping until golden.
- **STEP 4**
  Sprinkle over 25g plain flour, allow to cook for a couple of mins,
  shake over 2 tsp Worcestershire sauce, pour in 500ml lamb or
  chicken stock, then bring to the boil.
- **STEP 5**
  Stir in the stewing lamb and kidneys and 2 bay leaves, then turn
  off the heat.
- **STEP 6**
  Arrange 900g peeled and sliced potatoes on top of the meat, then
  drizzle with a little more dripping.
- **STEP 7**
  Cover, then place in the oven for about 1½ hrs until the potatoes
  are cooked.
- **STEP 8**

Remove the lid, brush the potatoes with a little more dripping, then turn the oven up to brown the potatoes, or finish under the grill for 5-8 mins until brown.

Arriving in the famous English seaside resort, Albert plans only to reminisce about a childhood holiday more than seventy years in the past. He will eat the town's most famous creation - the sugary treat known as Rock.

But when he walks into a shop being shaken down by heavies enforcing a protection racket, all thoughts of relaxation go out the window.

Instantly marked when Rex rousts the criminals, Albert must choose whether to leave the town – the sensible choice – or unravel the gang's plans – the option containing the greatest likelihood for mayhem and danger.

However, the choice is not his, because his partner has sniffed something other than cavity-inducing candy on the wind ...

... the scent of a wolf. A real one. And if Rex's nose is right, then it needs his help.

Man and dog both know how to solve a crime, but separated and working independently, can they arrive at the same conclusion? Can they be as effective working individually?

One thing is for certain.

There is going to be bloodshed.

A FREE Rex and Albert Story

There is no catch. There is no cost. You won't even be asked for an email address. I have a FREE Rex and Albert short story for you to read simply because I think it is fun and you deserve a cherry on top. If you have not yet already indulged, please type the link below into your web browser and read the fun short story about Rex and Albert, a ring, and a Hellcat.

https://stevehiggsbooks.com/hellcat-a-rex-and-albert-short-story/

When a former police dog knows the cat is guilty, what must he do to prove his case to the human he lives with?

His human is missing a ring. The dog knows the cat is guilty. Is the cat smarter than the pair of them?

A home invader. A thief. A cat. Is that one being or three? The dog knows but can he make his human listen?

When a climber suspiciously falls to his death and a local artist has her dog stolen, both cases fall into the lap of local sleuth, Patricia Fisher …

… but they should have come with a warning.

No sooner does she start to investigate, than a mysterious underworld figure issues a confusing threat. What has she uncovered?

Local boy, Sam Chalk, wants to help, his antics amusing but seemingly nothing more than a distraction. Does he know something though?

With time running out to save the dog, and the climber's death looking like nothing more than a terrible accident, a chance discovery will rock Patricia's world.

If only she had listened to Sam.

Marriage? It can be absolute murder.

Wedding planner for the rich and famous, Felicity Philips is aiming to land the biggest gig of her life – the next royal wedding. But there are a few obstacles in her way ...

... not least of which is a dead body the police believe she is responsible for murdering.

Out of custody, but under suspicion, her rivals are lining up to ruin her name. With so much on the line, she needs to prove it wasn't her and fast. But that means finding out who the real killer is ...

... without said killer finding out what she is up to.

With Buster the bulldog as her protector and Amber the ragdoll cat providing sartorial wit – mostly aimed at the dog - Felicity is turning sleuth.

What does a wedding planner know about solving a crime?

Nothing. Absolutely nothing.

Get ready for a wild ride!

More Books by Steve Higgs

Blue Moon Investigations

Paranormal Nonsense

The Phantom of Barker Mill

Amanda Harper Paranormal Detective

The Klowns of Kent

Dead Pirates of Cawsand

In the Doodoo With Voodoo

The Witches of East Malling

Crop Circles, Cows and Crazy Aliens

Whispers in the Rigging

Bloodlust Blonde – a short story

Paws of the Yeti

Under a Blue Moon – A Paranormal Detective Origin Story

Night Work

Lord Hale's Monster

The Herne Bay Howlers

Undead Incorporated

The Ghoul of Christmas Past

The Sandman

Jailhouse Golem

Shadow in the Mine

Patricia Fisher Cruise Mysteries

The Missing Sapphire of Zangrabar

The Kidnapped Bride

The Director's Cut

The Couple in Cabin 2124

Doctor Death

Murder on the Dancefloor

Mission for the Maharaja

A Sleuth and her Dachshund in Athens

The Maltese Parrot

No Place Like Home

Patricia Fisher Mystery Adventures

What Sam Knew

Solstice Goat

Recipe for Murder

A Banshee and a Bookshop

Diamonds, Dinner Jackets, and Death

Frozen Vengeance

Mug Shot

The Godmother

Murder is an Artform

Wonderful Weddings and Deadly Divorces

Dangerous Creatures

Patricia Fisher: Ship's Detective

Patricia Fisher: Ship's Detective

Albert Smith Culinary Capers

Pork Pie Pandemonium

Bakewell Tart Bludgeoning

Stilton Slaughter

Bedfordshire Clanger Calamity

Death of a Yorkshire Pudding

Cumberland Sausage Shocker

Arbroath Smokie Slaying

Dundee Cake Dispatch

Lancashire Hotpot Peril

Blackpool Rock Bloodshed

Felicity Philips Investigates

Real of False Gods

Made in the USA
Las Vegas, NV
15 November 2023